MACK

BOOK SIX OF THE ANGELBOUND OFFSPRING SERIES

CHRISTINA BAUER

COPYRIGHT

Monster House Books
Brighton, MA 02135
ISBN 9781946677532
First Edition

DEDICATION

**For All Those Who Kick Ass, Take Names
and Read Books**

CONTENTS

ALSO BY CHRISTINA BAUER

APPENDIX

1. Angelbound
2. Scala
3. Acca
4. Thrax
5. The Dark Lands
6. The Brutal Time
7. Armageddon
8. Quasi Redux
9. Clockwork Igni

Angelbound Lincoln

The Angelbound experience as told by Prince Lincoln

1. Duty Bound
2. Lincoln
3. Trickster
4. Baculum
5. Angelfire

Fairy Tales of the Magicorum

Modern fairy tales with sass, action, and romance

1. Wolves and Roses
2. Moonlight and Midtown
3. Shifters and Glyphs
4. Slippers and Thieves
5. Bandits and Ball Gowns
6. Fire and Cinder

7. Fairies and Frosting
8. Towers and Tithes
9. Evil Queens and Goblin Kings

Dimension Drift
Dystopian adventures with science, snark, and hot aliens
1. Scythe
2. Umbra
3. Alien Minds
4. ECHO Academy
5. Justice
6. Slate

Pixieland Diaries
About sassy pixie Calla and her love-crush-nemesis, the elf prince Dare
1. Pixieland Diaries
2. Calla
3. Dare
4. Winter Prince
5. Ley Queen

Beholder
Where a medieval farm girl discovers necromancy and true love
1. Cursed

This is a finished series.

MACK

KAPS

2:12 AM.

I wake up to find something strange in my bed. *That would be my boyfriend, Mack.* This is odd because my guy should be trapped in an entirely different world, namely Earth. Meanwhile I'm stuck in the dragon realm, Furonium.

Plus when I say he's *in my bed,* I mean Mack appears to be standing with his legs under my mattress and his torso above it. His body is also semi-transparent, like a ghost who's in full color.

And this isn't a dream.

I'm definitely awake because the rest of my bedroom looks like it always does. The decor is *modern prisoner chic.* There's a metal bed frame as well as an intricate wall-o-boxes that hold all my stuff. Other than that, I have a single steel chair and that's it. There are certainly no intra-realm portals hidden in my socks, that's for certain.

Which brings me back to Mack. Since he's here, there's clearly some magic at work. Not that I'm complaining.

Sitting up, I soak in the sight of him, from Mack's rumpled dark hair to his intelligent blue eyes and muscular body. How did he get in here, anyway? After all, I'm locked up in the most carefully-guarded tower in the dragon realm. There are literally a thousand warriors—and just as many magical wards—in place to keep people out.

And when I talk about *people*, I mostly mean Mack. Let's just say my parents—the Emperor and Empress of Furonium—aren't too thrilled that we're dating.

Yet Mack promised to find me. And here he is. My throat tightens with a combination of love and disbelief.

"Kaps? Can you hear me?"

"Yes." I smile so hard, my face hurts. Reaching forward, I go to pull Mack into an embrace. Sadly, my hand moves through his torso like he's made of smoke. I stifle a frown. Guess we're not getting touchy here.

"So glad I got through," says Mack. "I found enchanted pendant called an Amulet of Mercury. It's a pretty good communication spell, but I'm not sure how long it will last."

Important fact. Mack and I love enchanted relics. I'm a dragon shifter, so adoring treasure is just in my DNA. For Mack's part, he likes magical junk because he's simply that awesome.

"It's like this," continues Mack. "Ever since you got locked in your tower, I've been hunting for a magical key to set you loose… and I finally found one in the ruins of Port Royal." Mack holds up a silver ring with a skull and crossbones on it. "This is an escape band. It allows for a journey past any barrier."

Sign me up. "How do I get that thing?"

"I'll ask Gage to be delivery boy."

Which is brilliant. Gage is none other than the King of the L'Griffe, which is the dragon shifter mafia on Earth. Normally, Gage doesn't do favors for anyone, let alone a human like Mack. But this is a special situation. Gage happens to have a mega-crush on my sister, Huntress.

Mack rubs his neck. It's a move that means he's thinking stuff through. "Huntress still lives with you, right? Otherwise, Gage won't be on board."

"Huntress is my warden so that's a big *yes.*"

"Then he'll deliver the ring, no problem. As a dragon shifter, Gage is allowed in your realm."

Part of me is overjoyed with this news. I'm imprisoned in the Auric Badlands, which is only the most desolate spot in the entire dragon realm. This escape ring could give me and Mack a chance to start our lives together.

Which is totally great.

Okay, maybe there are a few issues.

Honestly? I have tons of questions.

"The ring is good for a single journey, correct?" I ask.

"Yes. The band allows you to pass by one barrier. You'll need to change into your dragon form and fly toward the portal for Earth. Right now, that gateway is locked to you. But with this ring, you can wing right through. You *can* sneak away from your tower, right?"

"Not at this exact moment, but I'll figure it out."

Mack shoots me a sly look. "That's my Kaps. Once you reach the portal, the ring will let you pass. It's a one-time, one-way trip."

Which is a great idea, except for, you know, *reality*. Mack has a lot going on. Leaning in, I take a closer look at my guy. Dark circles hang under his eyes. His hair appears matted and dull. Every line of his body seems to scream out for a nap. There's no question why Mack is exhausted, either. My guy runs the Zoetic, a league of vampire-hunting humans. It's a job he inherited when his old boss and mentor, Roman, turned traitor.

I may be stuck in the dragon realm, but I still get

snippets of news from Earth. Roman left things a mess. Mack is wearing himself down in order to build the Zoetic up.

I slap on what I hope is a casual tone. "How's life at the Fortress?"

"You know me," Mack replies. "I won't sugar-coat things. The Zoetic bank accounts are almost empty. The building is falling apart. And I have two hundred sick warriors who are only healthy enough to be constant pains in my ass. I was lucky to get away for the relic mission to Port Royal."

"So you aren't leaving the Fortress."

"Not until most of the Zoetic are fully healed. That's months from now."

"And Roman?"

"Our old Liege is in hiding." Mack's mouth thins to an angry line. "And it gets worse from there. Roman still plans to break into El Dorado, make more vampires for his army, and then erase all of humanity. I must get the Zoetic healed up so they can help stop him."

A long stretch of silence falls between us. Bands of sorrow tighten around my chest. *How I hate giving voice to this truth.*

"I can't go to you now," I explain. "If I left this tower, the first thing my parents would do is destroy your Fortress. I can't end the Zoetic, or place humanity at risk." *Among other things.* Not that I'll burden Mack with my sibling troubles. The man has enough on his plate.

"We can figure things out, Kaps. We're rhanas… Life mates."

"And we *will* make this work. Just not right now."

As Mack predicted, his communication spell starts to dissolve. One moment, Mack looks ghostly but in full color. The next second, his body appears in the barest shade of white.

Mack tilts his head. "What else aren't you telling me?"

I sigh. Not sure how Mack figured this out, but I have indeed been holding back. "It's my sister, Huntress. Ever since she met Gage, she's been in a serious depression. I can't leave until she's in better shape. And I won't go to you, only to tear down your world."

Mack's features take on an unreadable look. "And what would change that?"

"The power to sneak back and forth between realms." I gesture toward the escape ring. "I need something that's an *anytime pass* instead of a *one-way ticket.*"

"Then *that's* what I'll make happen." The vision of Mack fades so much, I can hardly tell he's in the room. "I'll find a way for us to be together, even if it's only for a few hours."

Some of the weight of sorrow lifts from my shoulders. "I know you will." *Or at least, you'll try.*

With that, Mack vanishes completely.

Now I'm not the kind of girl to sit around and wait for someone else to get my ass out of trouble. If Mack can find an escape ring, then I'll uncover some magic to allow that band to work more than once.

I grin. *Oh, how I do love a challenge.*

2

MACK

*A*fter my talk with Kaps, it takes me a while to fall asleep. And once I do conk out, I don't really get any rest. In my dreams, I chase vampires through a darkened forest while frogs croak out the song, *Everybody Was Kung Fu Fighting*.

I know, weird.

Ignoring the strangeness, I focus on catching vampires. Yet no matter how hard I try, I never get close enough to take one down. Talk about frustrating.

A new voice echoes through the night. "Mack."

Unlike the amphibian singers, this speaker sounds pretty real. Wouldn't be the first time someone had to wake me up before dawn.

Little by little, I force my eyes to open. I'm so out of it, I half expect vampires to leap through the stone walls of my medieval-style bedroom. Instead I find my best friend, Ndidi, standing beside my cot. Moonlight accents his brown eyes, strong cheekbones and ebony skin. He has a scowl on his face and a toilet brush gripped tightly in his fist.

Wait, a toilet WHAT?

Blinking hard, I try focusing my bleary mind. Once my head feels sharp, I shoot another glance in Ndidi's direction.

That's a toilet brush, all right.

"Are you awake, my Liege?" he asks.

Ndidi and I have been buddies since we were six years old. My friend hates waking me up, so he's throwing around this Liege stuff.

"Call me Mack," I counter.

"Fine." Ndidi leans in closer. "You look like Hell, *Mack*."

I chuckle. "That's more like it."

Ndidi's not lying, either. All in all, I resemble a nineteen-year-old after a week-long beer bender instead of the leader of an elite league of vampire hunters. Not that I'm surprised. People's lives depend on my decisions. With every choice, a little more of my soul seeps from the leaky bucket of my existence.

Drip... Drip... Drip...

Maybe that's a bit emo, but I'm nineteen and trying

to stop the world from getting destroyed by vampires. I figure I'm allowed a little drama.

Ndidi speaks, snapping me out of my thoughts. "What's the verdict?"

"Oh, you're still wondering about my face." I round on my friend. "Yeah, I look like Hell."

He winks. "Told ya."

I shoot Ndidi a frown, but there's no real anger in it. "What's up?"

Ndidi sighs. "Wish I had better news for you."

There's a reason everyone calls me Mako. It's because I have a shark-like ability to keep moving forward. In fact, it's my chilly and calculating side that kicks into high gear right now. An explanation for Ndidi's visit quickly appears.

"Don't tell me," I begin. "You're here because old Doc Langstrom is at it again."

My friend's eyes widen. "How did you know?"

"I was the only one who could stop Doc from bothering people with spatulas, couch cushions, and that box of ballbearings... and now you're holding a toilet brush. Call it a lucky guess. What's Langstrom doing?"

"The good doctor is roaming around the healing chamber, looking for magical relics. It took me an hour to get this so-called *wand of recovery* away from him." As he says the words *wand of recovery*, Ndidi waves the toilet brush around.

"And that's not an actual relic?"

True fact. Modern wizards rarely hide their powers in something so obvious as a cooly-cool wand. Today's magic users are more of a *hockey sticks and Pez dispensers* kind of crowd. I haven't seen an enchanted toilet brush before, but it's totally possible.

"This item is incredibly ordinary, if you get my meaning." Ndidi sniffs the brush and winces. "Doc was blessing the other patients with it. He'd bonk them on the head while saying *I heal thee.* Not okay. Folks need their rest."

"As well as basic hygiene," I state. "Doc is in the healing chamber, after all. He's supposed to be getting better, not spreading toilet brush funk around."

My people hunt the Audax, shape-shifting vampires that mimic their most recent victims. Right now, our healing chamber is filled with Zoetic who are recovering from a magical plague sent by our blood-sucking enemies. In fact, the top vampire boss—meaning the very Audax who was infecting our people—also ran the Zoetic at the same time. *Roman.*

Damn, do I ever hate that guy. Long story.

I haul on some jeans and a T-shirt. "I got this. Grab some sleep."

Ndidi nods and slogs off toward his bedroom. At the same time, I head for the healing chamber. The Fortress is always empty these days, but it's especially lonely at night. As I step through yet another empty stone passage, that's when it happens. Someone whispers in a voice that only I can hear. The message is always the same.

"Wyverns."

Ever since I was a kid, I've heard this phantom speaker.

"Wyverns."

Needless to say, I grew up obsessed with these creatures. Unlike dragons, Wyverns have wings that stretch between their arms and torsos, versus just hanging from their shoulders. No one's ever seen one in action, though. Wyverns disappeared more than a thousand years ago.

"Wyverns." *This is getting annoying.*

Good thing I recently found a way to make this voice shut its mystical yap. Pausing, I take in a deep breath and picture all the things I love about Kaps. There's her bright smile… the intelligent gleam in her whiskey-brown eyes… how she recklessly joins any kind of battle, whether it's verbal or demonic… And the way her kisses charge every cell in my body with desire.

Sure enough, the voice vanishes.

This trick works because Kaps is my mate—what dragon shifters call a rhana. I lift my hand. Kaps' escape ring sits on my pinky. I had such hopes for this band, but it's turned into a symbol of our broken future. Sorrow presses in around me. I hate to admit this, but Kaps is right. Even rhana magic has its limits.

Besides, what are the chances that I'll heal the Zoetic and defeat Roman? Slim to none. Not to mention how Kaps' family wants to kill me. That's a hard limit on our future.

At some point, I'll need to come to terms with a rough reality. Kaps can never be mine. And the sooner I set her loose, the better for us both.

3

KAPS

ONE MONTH LATER

*a*fter days of scheming, I come up with a scheme to turn Mack's escape ring into something far better. At the same time, I've decided to actively ignore the fact that I'm pretty sure we don't have a future together.

Denial, thy name is Kaps.

But back to my plan, since that bit is actually fun. My scheme centers on my secret lair. For years, I've kept a cave of magical goodies back at the imperial palace. Once I get in there, everything becomes more than simple. All I need is my magical smelting kit and a pair of enchanted rings I got from Morocco. From there, I just smush the two bands together into one Sauron-style master ring that extends the power of Mack's escape bling.

The easy part? Wearing two rings.

The tough stuff? Escaping my tower. Flying across Furonium. Breaking into my old lair. Finding the bands. Smelting stuff for hours on end. And doing all this without getting caught.

Long story short, this isn't easy. Fortunately, I have Huntress. The short cut for this situation is to talk my sister into helping me.

Turns out, breaking down Huntress takes three solid weeks of pleading. She finally agrees. After that follows one solid week of non-stop nudging, because my sister stalls on actually sneaking into the palace.

At last, off she goes.

Which brings me to the present moment. Any minute now, Huntress will walk through my bedroom door. If all goes to plan, then she'll have the new ring with her. I've decided to call it the Badass Booster because everything that is both super-cool and magical needs a good name.

To pass the time, I invest some quality brain cells in one of my ongoing obsessions. Why did Sauron name his band *the one ring?* Can you say, *phoning it in?* There are tons of good names out there. Like Excelsior. Apexium. Fred. Creating a master band to rule everyone is pretty complex stuff, so it's not like Sauron didn't have the IQ or drive to make this happen. Then again, this is the same dude who calls himself the Dark Lord. Maybe creativity is his thing.

The door creaks open, breaking up my thoughts. Huntress steps into the room and closes the door silently behind her. As always, a picture her elegant bone structure and intelligent eyes should be listed in a dictionary under the word, *regal*. This morning—like most days—Huntress pairs her dainty perfection with purple battle leathers.

But none of that is new.

One thing is, however: the look in Huntress' eyes. She appears more shocked than I've ever seen them before. Honestly, it's nice to see an expression other than absolute misery. And yes, I want me some lair love.

"Wow," whispers Huntress. "That's some lair you've got going."

"I know." I bob my brows. I've been waiting years for this reaction. No one has seen my secret lair before except my grandmother, a lady we all call Great M. Not to brag, but the design beats up the Bat Cave and calls it a bitch.

"You're really been busy."

Those are the words Huntress says, but I get the hidden meaning. My twin sister, Zinnia, was kidnapped when we were little. As a result, my parents got way overprotective. At the same time, I wanted to spend my life killing vampires and hunting down enchanted relics. So I made up a rock band and scheduled gigs wherever there was a vampire to stake or a trinket to find.

It worked great in one way. Namely, my parents let me do what I want. The not-so-nice part is how everyone thinks I'm a major screw up. That's what Huntress means by saying, *you've been busy.* She's shocked I could build and stock an awesome underground lair. This is a point I should probably let slide, but *nah.*

"You all thought I was a screw-up and—SURPRISE! —I'm not." I scooch to the edge of my bed. "Did you find the smelter?"

"I did. It's a cauldron with a dial on it, just like you said."

"And you set it at Sauron Seven level?" I made up the leveling system myself. Sauron Seven is the highest setting.

"Yup. Then I put in the two rings and made this." Huntress reaches into the pockets of her purple leathers and pulls out the ugliest band I've ever seen. The thing resembles more of a circle of silver and gold paint splatters than anything else.

If it works, it will be the most gorgeous creation ever.

Crossing the room, I take the ring from Huntress. It

looks solid enough. Reaching into the pocket of my leather jacket, I pull out a small cup-like amulet and a few gemstones. Time to test if this thing works.

Huntress moves to look over my shoulder. "What's that?"

"Some magical items from my lair."

"But I thought I was the only one who could get in there."

"Right now, you're the only one who can go in there for hours and hours. Smelting a ring takes forever, and I can't hang out that long without setting off a million magical alarms. But do I pop over super-fast and pick up a magical item or two? Sure."

While speaking, I set the ring onto the cup-style amulet and position the gemstones around it. If the Badass Booster works the way I planned, then these stones will light up once I get them in place.

"How do you escape the tower?" The way Huntress says those three worse, it's clear that I better come clean.

"Is this room warded against eavesdropping?"

"Obviously, or I wouldn't have brought in the ring and discussed it in the first place."

"Good point." I fiddle with the ring and stones a little more. "The key is to know the guard schedule. Some of our guards are the A team. Others? Not so much. If I know when the sloppy guards are around, I can sneak away. I just can't have anything metal on my body."

Huntress nods slowly. "Who's the Z team?"

"You'll figure it out on your own easily enough. And the metal thing is because Mum and Da had Mistress Cerys cast most of the protection spells on the tower. Cerys thinks no one will leave their home without wearing feathers or metal." If you knew Mistress Cerys, you'd understand.

At last, the tiny stones glow with white light. "Yay! It works!" I pull Huntress into a close embrace. "Thanks so much."

I set the janky band on my finger. Now that it's done, my heart sinks to my toes. I'd been so concerned about making this thing, I didn't think about whether or not I could use it to see Mack.

Pro tip: I can't.

Huntress purses her lips. "You don't seem happy."

"I'm thinking about Mack." I slip the ring into my pocket. "There's so much stacked against us. Plus Mack needs to save the world from freaking vampires. What kind of person would I be if I got in the way of that?"

"Rhana bonds are tricky," says Huntress. And as she speaks these words, it's as if every ounce of personality drains from my sister. "They are rare for a reason."

No question what huntress is thinking about now. Her

and Gage. And Huntress is miserable. Which makes me feel totally guilty for bringing up Mack to begin with. Maybe I can cheer up the conversation a little.

"Of we could look at it another way," I suggest. "After all, rhana bonds worked out well for Mum and Da."

"Our parents are the exception, not the rule."

And sadly enough, I fear that Huntress is right. I take the ring from my pocket and set it into the top drawer of my dresser.

If I truly love Mack, maybe I must let him go.

4

MACK

*H*as it only been a month since I last spoke to Kaps with the Amulet of Mercury? Feels like a million years. Plus, it doesn't help that I'm working from Roman's old study today. Talk about depressing.

The room itself is snug and wooden. The walls are lined with books and magical junk. And painful memories lurk in every corner. How many times did I come in here and seek Roman's advice? *Too many.* And all the while, Roman was plotting how his Audax vampires could strike down our Zoetic warriors.

What a sicko.

On the other side of the study door, a line of Zoetic wait for an audience with me, their new Liege. Without even seeing them, I can sense how each needy soul pulls a bit more from my internal reserves.

Drip... Drip... Drip...

It's my shark-side that makes me move forward and focus on the next Zoetic in line. Cupping my hand beside my mouth, I call out a single word. "Next."

The door opens to reveal a woman in a catsuit with the hood drawn low. It's Divya, one of the senior spies from our Cabal of Ghosts.

I gesture to the chair across from mine. "Have a seat."

"No, I'll stand. This room gives me the creeps." She inhales. "Smells funny, too. Like Roman on a bad body odor day. How do you stand it in here?"

"It's where all the records are," I explain. "And you get used to the smell."

"Well, I'd never be Zoetic Liege."

"I'm aware."

Most of my official office chats begin with some discussion about how I'm bat-shit crazy to take this job in the first place. Like I don't know that. Normally, Divya is one of the few who gets right down to business.

All of which means one thing.

I've a long day ahead of me.

ROMAN'S STUDY

5

MACK

The day from Hell continues.

Divya strolls past one of Roman's bookshelves while running her finger along the titles. "I don't know how you handle the pressure," she muses. "Roman could reappear at any time, you know."

I lean back in my stiff wooden chair. "Did you have an actual intelligence report for me? Because the fact that my job sucks is nothing new."

"Sure," says Divya. "I did turn up some info about Roman. He's waiting for the magical city of El Dorado to reopen. Once inside, Roman will create his ultimate weapon for wiping out humanity... a *new* Audax army."

It's no secret that Roman wants to destroy all humans. Once the guy figured out how to replicate blood, Roman decided that his vampire army should rule the Earth without the hassle of previous residents taking up all the good real estate. That said, another part of Divya's report is definitely a revelation.

"You said *new Audax*," I prompt.

"Roman calls them Toxicants."

"That sounds like a Roman name."

"These vampires are better, faster and stronger than regular Audax. Most importantly, it'll be much harder to tell them apart from the living."

I shake my head. "I can't imagine how Roman managed to pull that off. No one's improved glamour spells in ages."

Divya shrugs. "That's just Roman."

And Divya is right. Our old Liege doesn't just look like Albert Einstein; he thinks along the same lines as well. Inventing is simply part of Roman's soul… and so is some dark stuff that belongs in the *business end* of a sewer.

I shoot Divya a thumbs-up. "Keep at it."

The remaining Zoetic file in and out. Each one shares their concerns. I field questions about food supply, duty rosters, vampire uprisings and budget shortfalls.

The last in line is Cole, a thirteen-year-old with blond hair, acne and a great attitude. Unlike Divya, he wears jeans and a dark T-Shirt.

I nod in his direction. "Citizen Cole."

"My Liege." Cole bowls slightly at the waist. "I'm here to report on my work with relics. Four more crates were discovered in the sub-basement. I made an inventory, just as you asked." He sets a sheet of paper on my desk. I quickly scan the items. A handful leap off the long list.

Golden stakes — four
Chain mails of charisma — three
Daggers of smiting — two

"Apologies," says Cole, " I wasn't able to find anything that can extend magic."

"That's all right."

Although I know my future with Kaps may come to nothing, I still keep looking for some kind of magic to will extend the power of my escape ring. That kind of relic isn't here, but one final item on the list does catch my attention.

Amulet of Mercury — One

I tap the words. "This looks interesting."

Cole leans over to scan the sheet. "Yes, I thought you might want that one. You said you'd used it before."

"I have." *To chat with Kaps.*

Cole reaches into the pocket of his jeans. "Here it is." He hands the item over. Sure enough, it's a smooth disc of white stone with Roman lettering on it. *An Amulet of Mercury.* And the rock positively vibrates with magic.

I clasp the amulet in my hand, then set it into the top drawer of my desk. "Thanks, Cole. You never know when things like this will come in handy."

"My Liege." Cole bows and takes off.

After Cole's well and gone, I pull out one of Roman's old ledgers. The man is a homicidal maniac, but he kept good records on relics. Maybe if I look carefully enough, I'll find something useful.

Suddenly, the office door swings open to reveal a very awake Doc Langstrom. He's an older man with tanned skin and a circlet of white hair about his balding head. His patient gown hangs loose around him.

"Why are you out of bed?"

Every nerve ending in my body seems to go on alert, and for a simple reason. Doc's eyes flare with blue light. I've seen this effect before. That's Doc's angelic magic.

"I drank a potion in Madagascar once," says Doc. "Makes me see things sometimes. That's why I came here."

"All right, Doc. Why don't you come inside and sit down?"

Doc doesn't budge.

Rising, I cross the room and try to pull the man inside, but Doc won't move an inch. This is classic Doc Langstrom, by the way. When the guy doesn't want to move, it's like trying to shove a brick wall.

"Your princess has found a way to extend the power of your magic ring. You need to see her."

I sigh. "That's not easy, Doc. Sometimes the best thing you can do is let someone live in peace. She doesn't need my trouble."

Doc's eyes flare more brightly than ever before. "And who are you to decide such things?"

The words take my breath away. I hadn't thought about it from that perspective. Kaps and I always worked as a team before. Was I taking that away from us now?

Doc blinks hard. After a few seconds, his irises return to their normal shade of blue. "Roman? Is that you?"

"No, it's Mack."

Doc's shoulders hunch over. "How did I get in here?"

"I think you've been sleepwalking again." When it comes to Doc, that's really the best explanation all around. Wrapping my arm around Doc's shoulder, I gently guide him back to the healing chamber. After that, I return to my own bedroom.

I've a lot of thinking to do.

MACK

*I*t's past 3 AM when I come to my big decision. Chances are, Kaps is doing the same thing that I am. She's hiding her ring because she thinks it's what's best for me.

And perhaps it is.

The truth could be that we aren't meant to be together. Still, if the end is all there is, then how we reach it matters. Kaps and I need to decide this as a team. If nothing else, maybe it will give us some closure.

Rolling out of bed, I pull on a pair of old jeans and slog over to Roman's old office. From there, it's easy to take out the Amulet of Mercury and activate it.

Soon a misty version of Kaps appears in the office. I know that in reality, she's back in her tower and lying in bed. But to my eyes, she's a ghostly girl who sleeps atop

Roman's desk. The study has never looked better, in my opinion.

"You have a habit of waking me up in the middle of the night."

I chuckle. "Sorry about that."

Damn. Kaps looks so beautiful, even half-asleep. Maybe it's our rhana bond, but every corner of my soul craves her. How can we ever be apart?

"Something bothering you?" She sits up. "I mean, beyond Roman and the Zoetic."

"I've been thinking a lot about us. Once I came to a decision, I couldn't wait to tell you."

"And what's that?"

"I know you found some way to extend the magic on the escape ring. I came here to give you a choice. Do you want to see each other, even if it's just for a few hours?"

Kaps shakes her head. "Mack, this isn't easy."

"But now that I see you, I know the answer. We must be together again."

"I'm poison to you."

That does it. *Time to pull in the big guns.* "If we meet up, I'll bring a magical relic."

Now, it's Kaps' turn to chuckle. "You know me too well, Bounty Hunter."

"My kind always gets our woman. Two hours, that's all I ask."

She shoots me the side-eye. "Ninety minutes."

"One hour."

"Deal."

The image of Kaps starts to fade. This amulet is dying out far more quickly than the last one. Whatever I need to say, I better get it out before the connection dies.

"I'll send you a messa—"

But the image of Kaps vanishes before I get a chance to finish.

Only one thing to do now.

Call the King of the dragon shifter mafia.

Yet before I dial Gage, I need to think through a few details. Kaps has agreed to a visit. When is the best time and place for us to connect?

I pace around the study and consider my options. In terms of a time to meet, the middle of the night is probably best. It's far safer for Kaps to slip away while everyone's asleep.

But where to meet?

Kaps and I haven't dated for that long. I want every moment we share to be special. To begin with, that means avoiding Furonium. Nothing kills date night like your parents executing your boyfriend. And if Kaps visits Earth, then it should be for something unique that helps us unwind. Connect. Enjoy. My eyes widen as an idea hits me.

Enchanted battle training. Kaps will love it.

I nod once, the decision made. Pressing a few buttons, I dial Gage. The guy picks up on the first ring.

"It is 3:17 AM." Gage has a French accent, so the words come out more as *Eet eez tree seventeen A-M.*

"Come on. You rarely sleep."

"True." There's no missing the smirk in Gage's voice. "What do you need?"

"I have a transporter ring. I'd like you to deliver that to Kaps along with a message. *Please join me for enchanted battle training this Saturday at midnight.*"

A long pause follows before Gage answers. "Oui. This, I will do. Hold the ring in your right hand."

We've done this routine before. It's how Gage and I share small objects over space. Only before, it's been for bounty hunter gigs. I lift up my right palm, careful to place the silver escape ring in the center of my palm.

"Done," I announce. An electric sense of power fills the air. Magic. A moment later, the ring glows with blue light. Then it vanishes. "Did you get it?"

"Received," says Gage. "I shall deliver the ring and your message."

"Thanks." I start to hang up and then pause. "And once you reach the tower, say hello to *her* for me." In this case, *her* is Kaps' sister, Huntress.

"Saying hello is not an easy thing to do, mon ami. Every time I see Huntress, she tries to kill me."

And with that, the line goes dead. *Typical.* Gage often ends conversations with the equivalent of *Huntress will soon kill me, buh bye.*

Those two *really* need to work their shit out.

Setting my cell back into my pocket, I start the long march back to my bedroom. And with each step, I remind myself of one key fact.

Come Saturday, Kaps and I will be together again.

Yes.

7

KAPS

THE NEXT MORNING

oday I wear my battle leathers and a smile on my face. Behind me, my tail sways in a slow and happy rhythm. It's just after dawn—my favorite time of day—and I stand on the roof of my prison-tower.

Little by little, the sun peeps over the horizon line, casting a golden glow over the grim expanse of the Auric Badlands. A low hum sounds. My breath catches. There's no mistaking that particular tone. Any minute now, an enemy should appear on the landscape below.

Can't wait.

Flat and rocky ground stretches out before me. Here and there, tufts of rough grass cling to the earth. Dry wind brushes across my skin. A chorus of grunts sounds nearby. No question why, either. My personal guard wait a few yards back, and these warriors are none too happy about my situation. I get that I'm a princess and it's bad news if I fall six stories to my death.

But I'm also a dragon shifter. This girl has wings. *Sheesh.*

Ignoring the guards, I keep up my vigil. To this end, I kneel by the roof's edge while scanning the barren ground below. So far, there's nothing but red rock as far as the eye can see. Adrenaline pumps through my veins.

After all the drama with Mack last night, I need a distraction. And right now? An enemy is definitely heading for my secluded tower.

Bring them on.

KAPS

8

KAPS

*W*hile teetering on the roof's edge, I can't help but imagine the battle to come. Over the last two weeks, ogres have been attacking my tower. Sure, these lumbering giants aren't exactly the fastest movers or thinkers around. But when you're stuck in the same building twenty-four-seven, any battle is a fun one.

One of the more adventurous guards steps forward. "Princess Kaps, why don't you return to your chambers?

"Because someone is coming."

"We're in the middle of nowhere. There haven't been any visitors in days."

"Think I'm wrong? Ask Huntress."

The guard scans from left to right. "She's not here."

My sister, Huntress, is a glass dragon, so she can go

invisible at will. She also has the very cool ability to appear as if she's made of glass. Huntress also takes after her name. My sis can silently track down anyone, anywhere. So unless you've spent a lifetime getting punked by her invisible appearances, it's easy to think she's not around when she's actually standing nearby.

Sure enough, Huntress materializes beside me. My sister can conjure up any outfit she wants, but today Huntress wears her standard outfit of purple battle leathers.

Upon seeing my sister, the guards let out a series of full-throated gasps. Is that more than a little entertaining, especially after all the Kaps-doubting that was going on?

You bet your ass it is.

Huntress surveys the guards with an empty stare. "Kaps is right."

A more mature prisoner would keep her mouth shut right now. Good thing I'm only eighteen.

"Nyah," I state regally.

With her entrance over, Huntress moves to stare blankly at the horizon line. Sorrow seems to pour off her in waves. My sister is having a bad morning. Fighting your rhana bond is a bitch. I should know. I've been doing it myself.

I slap on a smile. "Missed you at breakfast."

Huntress doesn't look in my direction. Doesn't even blink, as a matter of fact. There's only the barest shrug of her shoulders.

Guess that's all the answer I'm going to get.

I lower my voice to a tone that only Huntress can hear. "You can just leave me for a little bit, you know. Go see Gage."

A wisp of a smile curls Huntress' mouth. Clearly, she's considering the idea. Every once in a while, Huntress will agree to visiting Earth. Sadly, she never follows through.

And I can't blame her. In my sister's opinion, she's the Imperial Enforcer for my parents. That means it's her job to follow every rule. Dating a criminal isn't exactly consistent with that life plan. It's a rough situation.

And the few times Huntress does run into Gage? That's when the fireworks start. And she's a happy girl for at least two weeks after.

Considering the sad vibe on this roof, I decide that a change of topic is definitely in order. "I'm thinking that an ogre horde is headed our way. Do you hear that high-pitched grumble? Sounds like their battle wagons. What's your guess?"

Huntress nods slowly. "Ogres made sense."

The slightest of grumbling noises echo through the

air. The sound is so faint, only Huntress and I catch it. My pulse speeds.

Ogre fun, yeah!

As my grandmother says, *it's almost time to kick ass and take names.* Sadly, my Great M is off on another one of her missions to save the after-realms. It would be sweet to share this fight with her.

The sound grows even louder. The guards all stiffen their stances. Now they hear that something is coming as well. But at this volume, it's clear to me that this noise isn't found in nature. It's mechanical.

"What *is* that?" asks Huntress.

"We'll know in a few minutes," I reply.

And I smile because I know something Huntress does not.

Gage Beaumont is on his way.

9

KAPS

*O*ff near the horizon line, a tiny plume of dust billows toward the sky. Soon the reason for the sight becomes clear. A line of stretch Bentleys tool across the Auric Badlands.

Not an easy thing to do.

As the vehicles get closer, it's clear that a dagger emblem adorns the grille of every carf. This isn't just any convoy.

It's Gage and his entourage. *Called it.*

The vehicle stop by the tower's main entrance. Gage steps out from the front ride. Like always, the guy looks like he fell of the cover of a couture magazine, what with his trim frame, dark hair and Armani suit. His blue tail sways behind him in a predatory rhythm.

Gage pauses near the front door.

Turning, I scan the guards behind me. All of them stare in rapt attention at Gage. No one makes a move to approach or stop him. There are two reasons for this.

First, Gage is a dragon shifter. Any of our people can approach royalty. Even here in the Auric Badlands, we've had tourists show up for a glimpse of the bad-girl princess (that would be me).

Second, Gage is dragon shifter royalty in his own right. Most of my people never leave Furonium. But Gage not only lives on Earth, he's also a badass crime lord. Right or not, that gives him outlaw celebrity status in Furonium. The last time Gage showed up, a few Kathikon asked for his autograph.

I swing my gaze toward Huntress. She's still visible and maintaining her stare fest with the skyline. Thus begins a kind of play that always happens when Gage shows up.

The story goes something like this. Once upon a time, there was a dragon shifter named Gage, a guy with a magnetic pull over his chosen lady, Huntress. The pull is bad twenty-four-seven, but it gets downright irresistible when Huntress becomes invisible. So when Gage is around, Huntress spends a lot of time trying *not* to go glassy, but that never lasts for long. Once Huntress turns invisible, then everything goes to Hell. Then end.

For my part, I've zero plans to pretend Gage isn't

around. So I leap down from roof, taking care to land before Gage. The moment my feet touch the ground, more Kathikon guards march out from the front gate. They move in single file to form a semi-circle around me, Gage and all his Bentleys.

"Bonjour." Gage's French accent is adorable.

"Hey, Gage. I'd ask you to come inside but it's not allowed."

"I appreciate the sentiment." He looks me over. "You seem ready for battle."

"You approached the tower with magically souped-up Bentleys. If I'm not mistaken, then these vehicles are enchanted to sound like an ogre horde. It's like you're trying to get attacked."

"Who knows?"

"I do. You so want to get tackled by Huntress, it isn't even funny." Stepping closer, I take care to lower my voice."Any messages for me?"

"Mmm." Gage taps his lips, like he's trying to remember why he came here in the first place. The guy can be such a dick sometimes.

"Come on, I know there's something for me from Mack."

"Oui. Lean in and I'll tell you a secret."

"Fine. I play along." When Gage gets close, he

pretends to shake my hand, but actually slips me a small round object.

The escape ring. Yes!

"Saturday. Midnight. Zoetic Fortress grounds. A battle training simulation for two. You understand?"

"Yup." In my mind, I say that word all suave-like. In reality, it comes out as more of a chirp than anything else. I have it so bad for Mack, it's not even funny.

Gage winks. "And so, a new era begins. Where you sneak around the Earth again."

"Only I won't have so many vampires to kill this time."

Gage nods toward my fist. "Will the guards take that away from you?"

"Nah, I'm allowed small gifts. And since it's from you, they'll definitely be cool with it."

"Me? Why?"

"You're a combination of outlaw and rock star here in Furonium. Don't tell me you aren't aware."

"I am not."

"Well, you could take a dump on my head and the guards would ask if they can have it as a keepsake."

"Quelle horreur."

A long moment passes where both wait for Huntress to do her thing. That doesn't happen. Craning my neck, I scan the roof once more. Sure enough, Huntress is still there, visible and miserable.

No point dragging this out. I take a pointed step backward. "Thanks, Gage. See you soon."

My words drive an immediate reaction from my sister. Huntress transforms from solid and visible into her glassy form.

Gage grins. Reaching into his suit jacket, the mafia king pulls out an ornate dagger. In a formal movement, he kneels and sets the blade onto the ground before him. It's a familiar-looking weapon, considering how it's the one Huntress bequeathed to Gage the first time she tried to kill him.

And yes, I said *first time.* These murder attempts are an ongoing theme.

Gage steps away from the blade.

I count down in my mind. *Three, two, one...*

The glassy version of Huntress leaps down from the roof and lands nearby. I can't catch her specific movements, but there's no missing the rush of wind as she speeds past, scoops up the dagger and then tackles Gage back-first onto the ground.

A moment later, Huntress becomes perfectly visible again. Only this time, she's straddling Gage with the dagger against his throat.

All the while, the Kathikon guard watch everything with interest. The first time Huntress did this, everyone lost their minds. Now folks just hang back, silent and wary.

Gage may be laying on his back on the dirt, but that satisfied grin stays firmly in place. For her part, Huntress leans in to sniff his neck. It might seem like a somewhat friendly move, but there's no missing how Huntress keeps the weapon pressed against Gage's throat.

Did I mention this is strange stuff? It is.

I'd look away for privacy's sake, but I don't trust whatever's happening here. As long as knives are in the mix, I'm keeping an eye on my sister.

Little by little, Huntress brushes her lips against Gage's mouth. Their kiss deepens. While they keep on smooching, Gage holds out his hand, palm upward. It's a clear signal for, *gimme.*

Sure enough, Huntress sets hilt of blade onto his palm.

For some reason, that movement always marks the end of this… *whatever it is.* Huntress gets up, grins and saunters back into the castle.

That is some whacked out shizz.

After Huntress is gone, I refocus on Gage. The man hops to his feet. The strong lines of his handsome face are pulled into an expression that can only be described as *blissed out*.

"What you two have is…" I smack my lips, trying to find the words.

"Parfaitement. Love is unexpected, non?"

His words make me think of Mack. "You've got that right."

"See you soon, Cherie."

The king climbs back into his fancy pants car and tools away. I sense more than see Huntress nearby, watching the scene with a smile.

As Gage's Bentley gets smaller on the horizon, a new sense of joy bubbles through me. *I'll see Mack Saturday.* In the meantime, all I must do is plan an hour-long escape from my tower.

Now that's what you call a labor of love.

ZOETIC FORTRESS

10

MACK

SATURDAY

*M*idnight is here.

Finally.

I stand outside the Zoetic Fortress with joy in my heart and a short sword in my fist. I think back to the toilet brush Doc Langstrom insisted was a magic wand. Unlike that cleaning item, this weapon is packed with spells.

Why the enchanted blade? Midnight is almost here and with it, Kaps. Once my girlfriend arrives, we'll hone our vampire hunting skills with the magical battle simulations loaded inside this very sword.

Stepping in a slow circle, I inspect the landscape. *Where should I wave this thing?*

There's no lack of places to cast, that's for certain. The full moon shows off every detail of the Fortress grounds. Essentially the place is a series of mini-castles and clusters of trees., all of which encircle a central lawn.

Nodding once, I make my decision. *Best to wave my sword-wand right in the middle of the open green.*

Turning, I march toward the lawn's center. Suddenly, a black shape passes over the moon. Pausing, I scan the dark streak more closely. To regular humans, that's an ordinary shadow. But I've a bit of demonic DNA in my background. Which means I can look past magical glamours.

To me, it's a dragon.

My grin widens. That's not just any dragon, either. It's Kaps. *The woman I love.* Based on her speed, she'll land any second.

Perfect.

A great black shape blots out the moon entirely. Massive dark wings send a gust of wind in my direction. Heat radiates from her dragon's body as Kaps lands only a few yards away. For a moment, I can soak in the glory of her form. Dark scales. Eyes that glow red. A line of scarlet spikes that run down her back and tail.

A shimmer of crimson light surrounds her body. For one more moment, the massive dragon looms before me. Then it's replaced by the human version of Kaps. My woman is no less impressive this way, what with her dark hair, amber eyes and whip-fast tail. She wears leather pants, hefty boots and a halter top.

Damn, I've missed her.

For my part, I sport black body armor. Unlike Kaps, I can't change my skin into dragon scales during battle. One of the many downsides of being human.

We close the space between us. Kaps moves to kiss me and pauses. A frown crosses Kaps' mouth. She erases the expression quickly enough, but I still caught it. And I know what's bothering her, too.

"I know," I declare. "I look terrible."

"What can I do to help?"

"Fight some vampires with me." I'd be subtle, but Kaps isn't that girl. She appreciates honesty above all else. It's one of the many reasons why I'm crazy about her.

"Will some kissing be involved eventually?"

"Most definitely. But not with the vampires."

"In that case, you have a deal." Kaps scans my hand. "Wait, what's with the sword?" A sly look shines in her eyes. She knows this thing isn't what it seems.

My dragon woman loves herself some treasure.

"It's a magic wand," I reply.

"Nostra Quattro made that for you, didn't he?"

I told Kaps all about our training program and the

wizards who make our stuff. It's how I knew she'd love this idea in the first place.

"That he did. Only the best for you, Kaps."

She winks. "So when do we start? I only have an hour, and I want to be sure we save time for kissing."

"Great thinking." This isn't my first time using a magic wand from Nostra Quattro. To launch the simulation, I wave the item while picturing the wizard who made it. Sure enough, that combination of action and imagery launches the spell. Mist pours out from the sword's end. The magical haze churns and thickens as it transforms into a humanoid shape.

From there, the cloud of power turns into something solid. That would be Nostradamus the Fourth, AKA Nostra Quattro. He's a classic-looking wizard, what with his long robes and full beard. That said, he's also a total hustler. If Nostra Quattro is showing up in person, then it's not to hand out extra spells and sing Kumbaya.

Kaps shoots me the side-eye. "Is that supposed to happen?"

"Ah, no. Waving the sword should just start a battle simulation, not summon the wizard behind the spell."

"So what do we do?"

"Talk to him," I reply. "Oh, and while we do that, keep your hand on your wallet or any valuables."

Kaps bobs on the balls of her feet. "This is getting good."

In this moment, energy pours off Kaps in waves. I can't help but smile. Here's what I've missed so much—the simple act of having a true partner to share things with.

"Yes, Kaps. Let's have some fun."

MACK

11

MACK

*I*f you asked a costume company for a warlock outfit, they'd probably send you what Nostradamus the Fourth is wearing right now. A long dark cape drapes over his shoulders. A tall staff is gripped in his right fist. The costume company might also send you a wrinkly mask and fake beard, too. But with Nostra Quattro, that stuff comes naturally.

There's no question why the Nostra Quattro dresses like a classic wizard, either. The man is a total hustler... and cons work better when you look the part. Don't get me wrong; Nostra Quattro can cast great spells. He's just constantly working an angle, that's all.

"Greetings, Liege Mack." Nostra Quattro bows slightly at the waist. "And Princess Kaps."

I get right to the point. "When I saw the specifications for this magic wand, I don't remember asking you to show up when I waved it."

"I did enhance things," says the wizard solemnly. "Considering all the changes here in the Fortress, I wanted to appear in person. I haven't seen you since you became Liege. Allow me to express my amazement at your great achievement."

And now we get to the *hustling part* of the conversation. It always happens with Nostra Quattro.

"You're here for a reason," I state. "And it's not to congratulate me on becoming Liege. What do you want?"

Nostra Quattro runs his wrinkly fingers through his long beard. It's a motion that's meant to appear as if the wizard were thinking about his question for the first time. The guy is so full of it.

"For decades, I have created battle simulations for the Zoetic. And make no mistake, this sword-wand will run you through a helpful training scenario. Still, I always put in an extra back door for more magic, just in case it's needed."

"Did Liege Roman ever pay you extra for these so-called *back door spells*?" I ask.

"Twice." When Nostra Quattro next speaks, he takes care to seem super-casual. That's how I know he's going for the close. "I always include an option to have the battle simulations include information about whatever the Zoetic Liege most needs to know."

Damn. Now I'm interested. I've been looking for intel on Roman. If this spell can help me, that's almost too good to pass up.

Kaps sets her fist on her hip. "What will happen?"

Nostra Quattro waves his arms dramatically. "You'll receive a seer spell of immense power. I don't know what it will display, but I can guarantee that it will be real."

I roll my eyes. *What a drama wizard.* "And how much will that cost?"

"The rest of your healing serum."

Huh. If Nostra Quattro wants some healing elixir, all the wizard has to do is ask. If I had any extra, I'd share it.

But I don't.

"I still have Zoetic in recovery. We need every dose."

Nostra Quattro grips his beard so tightly, I'm surprised he doesn't pull out a handful. "Then replicate some for me."

I shake my head. "I didn't get that much from the Halcyon coven to begin with. If I stretched it out any more, the serum wouldn't work. I won't sell you bad goods."

An anxious gleam shows in Nostra Quattro's eyes. "What if I have the wand go through two scenarios instead of one? That way, you'll definitely learn something useful."

I sigh. "I still can't give up any serum."

Kaps reaches into her pocket and pulls out a small loop of bone. "I've got a vitality wrist cuff. Will that do?"

My eyes widen. *My woman is brilliant.* Healing magic can do more than help the sick. On the healthy, it also restores youth.

Nostra Quattro narrows his eyes. "That wrist cuff doesn't create a glamour? It actually makes you young?"

"Sure, as long as you keep it on. I have other ones that are metal, but I couldn't take them with me tonight. But this one has carvings on it. Pretty, so long as the bone-thing doesn't bother you."

"It doesn't." Nostra Quattro makes grabby hands at Kaps. "We have a bargain."

Kaps looks to me. "Do you trust him enough for me to toss this over?"

"I do."

Kaps chucks the wrist cuff at Nostra Quattro. He catches the item, sets it into the folds of his cloak, and shoots a doe-eyed look at no one in particular. All of a sudden, I understand what this is about.

"Who do you want to be young for?" I ask. Wizards aren't the type who care for looks, as a rule. But love makes you do crazy things.

"That obvious, eh?" Nostra Quattro blushes. "I may have fallen in love with a young human."

"Good for you." Kaps shoots him a thumbs-up.

Nostra Quattro bows slightly at the waist. "Now if you don't mind, I must be on my way."

"Hey, there." I lift the sword-wand. "Don't you need to open the back door on this thing first?"

"Ah, yes," replies the wizard. "Almost forgot."

Sure, he did.

Twisting about, Nostra Quattro points his staff in my direction. A moment later, lightning bolts pour off the round stone at the scepter's end… and land right onto the sword-wand in my grasp. The blade soaks in magic until it glows red with power.

"Now," states Nostra Quattro. "Wave the wand with intent."

That means that I must picture what I want the spell to do. Closing my eyes, I move the sword while imagining Foman. For a long moment, the weapon keeps flaring with magical light.

Then everything changes.

Tendrils of smoke and light burst from the end of the sword-wand, shooting off in a thousand directions at once. Then all the Fortress grounds turn thick with white haze. A wind strikes up with such force, the gusts moan like voices.

I pull Kaps against my side. "Sorry," I whisper. "This was supposed to be fun."

She kisses my cheek. "Are you kidding? I've been locked in a tower. This is the best time I've had in weeks."

I can't help but smile. "Good. So you know, it's an illusion that's just for the two of us."

The long cords of pale magic burrow into the ground. The earth shimmies with power. It's a good thing that this simulation only affects me and Kaps. Otherwise I'd have hundreds of Zoetic freaking out on the lawn. The ground rumbles with more magic than ever before.

Then the earth rips open.

The Fortress collapses. Grey bricks tumble to the ground. Ear-piercing booms rattle the air.

Kaps gives me the side-eye. "Is this supposed to happen?"

"Sort of," I reply. "Nostra Quattro is an expert at realistic illusions. Normally his spells build up a room or two. I've never seen this much destruction before."

Cords of white energy twist through the stones that once made up the Fortress proper, yanking them apart and placing them together in a new way. At the same time, the Fortress grounds change as well. Palm trees jut up from the earth. Hanging vines twist between the branches. A wet heat fills the air. Within seconds, we stand with a massive jungle behind us and an elaborate city before our eyes.

A chorus of loud snaps sounds as the massive city complex pulls apart into two sections. With a roar of rushing water, a great river flows between the two halves of the city. From there, the liquid rolls out into the jungle beyond.

Everything falls quiet.

The moon slowly rises over the scene, casting everything in shadows. Still there's no mistaking the simulation that Nostra Quattro created for us.

It's the lost city of El Dorado.

MACK

Kaps laces her fingers with mine. Together, she and I soak in the beauty of this simulated city. I can't imagine any place that's more lovely.

The moon vanishes while the sun rises.

Bright light floods the scene. With this extra brightness, it's clear that this isn't a place built of brick. Every inch of El Dorado gleams with gold. Even the river that moves through the city's center appears to be liquid metal.

All Wyverns have the power to fly and flight. Yet only the king and queen breathe the magical fire that's called the Breath of Midas. This flame not only burns, it also transforms anything into gold. Clearly, that's what happened here.

Kaps lets out a low whistle. "You sure know how to make date night special."

More white tendrils of magic twist over the city walls, creating a tall gate that swings open. Next the magic goes to work on the ground before the gate itself, turning chunks of grass into golden stones. Soon, there's a gleaming pathway from the city that ends right under our feet.

I step around in a slow circle. No signs remain of the white magic tendrils that are Nostra Quattro's trademark. The spell is over. I focus on Kaps.

"Are you thinking what I'm thinking?" I ask.

"We are *so* exploring this city."

Hand in hand, Kaps and I stroll through the gates of El Dorado. Once inside, we find that the narrow streets are also paved with gold. Small stalls line the walkways. It's some kind of open market.

Overhead, Wyverns wheel through the blue skies. Down in the city, only people stroll across the ground. Which isn't a surprise, considering how Wyverns can change forms just like dragon shifters.

It's what everyone's wearing that's a shock.

Back in the Zoetic library, we have an encyclopedia about ancient Greece. Entering the City of El Dorado is like stepping back into the pictures of that book. Both women and men wear long togas. Everyone sports curly hair and sandals.

Kaps and I walk past the various stalls. It's pretty typical stuff. Apples. Spices. Dried meats. One table has carved busts of what I assume are famous people. All of them are in gold, of course.

Kaps points to a nearby head. "That one looks like you."

I step up for a closer look... meaning I walk right through a few locals who surround the stall. This is how Nostra Quattro's simulations always work. The people in them can't detect us. *Unless we're supposed to kill them, of course.* In that case, the simulated person sees us and how.

Leaning in, I examine a small carving. Sure enough, it does look a bit like me. The inscription on the bottom reads, Vasiliás IX.

A memory knocks around the back of my head. I've seen the word Vasiliás before. Maybe in the Zoetic library? I'm almost about to recall when a great cry echoes down the city streets. The crowd chants in unison.

"Lady Aurelian! Lady Aurelian!"

My skin prickles over with gooseflesh. Kaps tightens her grip on my hand. Lady Aurelian is the last Queen of

El Dorado. She not only wields the Breath of Midas, but she's also a great enchantress.

Lady Aurelian steps through the streets. She wears a black toga that's fringed in gold. Her features are even and timeless, from her wide mouth and brown hair to her intelligent blue eyes. There's even a sheen to her skin that makes her seem more mannequin than human. This woman may be called a queen, but to me, she looks more like a goddess.

Suddenly, dark clouds roll over the skies. Monstrous shrieks fill the air. The people in the streets start to scream.

"The prophecy is coming true!" cries one. "Vision and the Darkness are coming!"

My heart sinks. This is my least favorite part of the El Dorado story. The beauty of the Wyvern world attracts two demon-titans, Vision and the Darkness.

And soon, they'll destroy everything.

For her part, Lady Aurelian hoists her skirts and races across the city. Kaps and I follow as well. The queen races up the steps to the tallest spire in El Dorado. Her guards stay close around her.

The queen halts at the peak of the tower. It's a snug space with a wooden floor and thin windows. A pair of small torches light up the room. This spot is meant to be a look-out more than anything else—the Wyverns haven't even bothered to turn the interior into gold.

Lady Aurelian races to a small window and looks out. Kaps and I do the same. From this height, we watch the rolling clouds as they cast long shadows over the vibrant jungle. Wherever shade falls onto the greenery, screams rise up from people and animals alike.

Vision and the Darkness are closing in on El Dorado. And as they move in, the demon-titans are killing everything in their path.

Lady Aurelian holds out her arm. Golden light glows on her palm. When the brightness dies down, the queen now holds a scepter in her hand. She points the staff at the approaching clouds. Golden light blasts out from the end of her scepter. *Magic.* Waves of colored power careen from the staff and slam right into the oncoming enemy.

Nothing happens.

The rolling darkness doesn't slow. Screams still sound from the countryside below. Again and again, the queen sends magical volleys toward the oncoming titans. If anything, the dark clouds only move faster in response.

Suddenly, the torches in the small chamber go out. Inky darkness surrounds us. The city outside also falls into unnatural black. A chill wind blows into the small room. Every nerve ending in my body goes on alert.

The demon-titans have reached the city.

The torches flare back to life. A pair of monsters now stand in the small room. One has a woman's body topped by an insect-like head. A pair of bat wings arch behind her. That's Vision. The only sign of the Darkness is a pair of glowing eyes that stare out from the shadows. A sense of evil intent rolls off the hidden creature.

I take a half-step forward. Neither Vision nor the Darkness seem to notice me. Which means these monsters aren't our foes for this simulation. I'd grabbed my dagger before; now I slowly reset the weapon into its holster.

Now that the immediate threat is gone, all my years of research come to mind. How many times did I read the few books on Wyverns? And How often did I endure those whispers? I've spent countless hours wondering what happened to El Dorado and its people. At last, I'll get a few answers. Even better, I can share the discovery with Kaps, who has my same obsession. And if it helps me stop Roman? So much the better.

Talk about a good simulation spell. Nostra Quattro should have held out for double payment.

VISION AND THE DARKNESS

13

KAPS

*T*his. Is. Awesome.

I don't know what I expected when Gage told me about a *battle training simulation for two.* But now my lifelong obsession with Wyverns is paying off. Color me happy.

"I address the Wyvern queen," says Vision. Her voice is low and scratchy. "I have moved across your countryside with the Darkness. Wherever we've touched, all your people there are dead. Surrender your city. You can't kill us."

Lady Aurelian grips her staff more rightly. "If you could take the city, you would have already. You fear my power at closer range."

"Does that mean you will try to kill us?" asks Vision.

A small smile rounds the queen's mouth. "That's not my plan at all."

Lady Aurelian slams her scepter onto the floor. Waves of golden light fan out from the spot. The motion reminds me of concentric circles on the surface of still water. All of a sudden, the floor gyrates.

I stumble over to a window. Mack stays at my side. Looking out, we see the entire city is covered in what looks like a golden dome. My mouth falls open in shock.

"She isn't," I whisper.

"She is." Mack wraps his arm around my waist. "Get ready for a bumpy ride."

I've heard of encapsulation spells, but I've never actually seen one performed before. In this kind of magic, a person or place is wrapped up inside a bubble and moved somewhere else.

I pull my brows together. "It doesn't make sense. Why encapsulate the city with Vision and the Darkness inside?"

"Check that out." Mack points to the distance. Some of the jungle has been caught up in Lady Aurelian's bubble. Now a smaller sphere of golden light hovers above a faraway stretch green.

"Clever," I state. "She's got another encapsulation spell at the ready."

"And it's just the right size to hold Vision and the Darkness."

The bubbled-up city rises far above the Earth. Only we're not above a jungle anymore. I gasp. I'd know the stretch of land below me like it was my own face.

"That's the Auric Badlands," I state. "It's where I've been living."

Mack angles his body for a better look. "And over there, you can see the only remnant of El Dorado. It's your tower."

My eyes widen. "El Dorado... Auric... Aurelian... they all mean gold. I've been living on the site of the old Wyvern homeland and I didn't even know it."

Mack sniffs. "Are you surprised? Most of Furonium —and all of Earth—fail to believe that Wyverns ever existed."

The bubble city now speeds toward the ground. I slide my arm around Mack's waist. This impact isn't going to be fun.

BOOM!

The encapsulated city slams into the earth. Howls of fear turn deafeningly loud. Around us, the golden light flares more brightly, then fades to darkness. Silence descends.

"Where are we?" I ask.

"Another dimension. That flare of magic was pretty intense."

Turning around, I scan the small room. Vision and the Darkness are gone.

Lady Aurelian sighs. She looks about a decade older. A few streaks of grey now highlight her once-dark hair. "Let's get down to the streets," the queen tells her guard. "We must check on the people."

The queen races down to the street below. Mack and I stay close behind. Once there, Lady Aurelian looks in on different citizens. Some need healing. Others try to drink from the dark waters that now flow through the city.

"Stop!" cries Lady Aurelian. "The water is now poisoned with the magic of Vision and the Darkness. We will provide you safe things to drink soon enough."

Once she's certain that the city is safe, Lady Aurelian marches out into the jungle. Her destination? The very spot where Mack pointed out the smaller encapsulation sphere.

We're about to discover what happened to Vision and the Darkness.

After what feels like hours of slogging along, we finally reach the place of the golden sphere. Only now, the bubble is gone. In its spot, there looms a massive mountain with a single entrance, which is a skull-like head with opened jaws.

Lady Aurelian slams her staff onto the ground once more. The stone head closes its mouth. "There. I did it. Vision and the Darkness are now imprisoned."

A guard steps up. "I'm sorry, your Majesty. Where are the demon-titans exactly?"

"Their dungeon is a great cavern inside this mountain," answers the queen. She gestures to the closed mouth entrance. "If you go into the mountain and pass through, you will reach Earth. That is now our only connection to the outside world.

The guard pales. "How can that be? You've cut us off from everyone. We'll die here."

I raise my hand. "You could have died ten minutes ago when Vision and the Darkness showed up." Sadly, the guard can't hear me.

Lady Aurelian leans on her staff. I'm pretty sure the thing is all that's keeping her upright. "Once every fifteen years, Vision and Darkness will sleep… for one hour only. It's all I can do. Over on Earth, a gateway will appear. The Divide. My magic will lure humans through that portal and into our world. The ones who answer the call will only be those who can bring us what we most need. Medicine. Seeds. Food. That's all I can do."

"Wow," I say in an extra-loud voice. "That's totally helpful. Thank you."

Mack shoots me a sly look. "She can't hear you. This is just a recreation of the past."

"I know. Still, I felt like someone ought to say it."

Suddenly, everything changes once more. They sky wheels overhead. Trees grow heavy with leaves only to turn bare and die.

Mack's forehead crumples with confusion. "What's happening?"

"Magic is showing us the passage of time. I've seen it before."

"Where?"

"Human movies. I have a collection back in my lair."

"Very cool. When this is all over, I want movie night at your place."

"Deal." Yet even as the word leaves my mouth, I know it's not true. Mack and I could barely agree to sneaking off and seeing each other for an hour. What kind of future do we really have?

Suddenly, the skies stop acting freaky. The trees cease to grow and die.

"Looks like time is done passing," deadpans Mack.

"If my guess is right, then we're fifteen years ahead."

Sure enough, the skull mouth opens its jaws. Humans wearing togas step out onto the green.

Wyverns walk out of the line of trees and approach the newcomers. Like the humans, the Wyverns are in two-legged form and sporting a toga.

"Welcome to El Dorado," says one Wyvern. "Magic chose you to come here."

Some chatter follows before the humans happily follow the Wyverns into the trees. My guess is that they're heading off to El Dorado.

The process then repeats. The skies wheel overhead. Grass grows and dies. Time passes. The skull mouth opens once more. More humans walk through. First there are folks wearing furs. Then come medieval knights and ladies. After that, a group of Victorian explorers in their pith helmets and overly-huge hairdos.

In each case, the Wyverns come out from the trees, greet the newcomers and lead them to El Dorado.

I'm starting to wonder why the spell is showing us every freaking group that walks out of the skull when it happens.

A group of Nazis march out onto the green. My blood freezes. Roman leads these warriors. The wisps of grey at his temples are the only sign of the Albert Einstein-style mess the guy would become.

Lady Aurelian approaches Roman. "My magic drew you here. Welcome."

"I'm not here for you," snaps Roman. "We need your

water. My people are in the middle of a war. I found some relics that led me to this spot. You have dark water. It's the key to our victory." Roman spots a puddle across the open green. He speeds over, kneels down, and fills his canteen.

While Roman does his thing, Lady Aurelian speaks to the other Nazis. Most ignore her, but one steps away.

Roman leaps to his feet. "Lucas! Get back here!"

But by this point, the Nazi named Lucas is deep under the cover of trees.

Beside me, Mack pales. I sense our rhana bond come to life between us. Suddenly, a golden glow dances above Mack's skin.

What's happening?

Lady Aurelian marches over to Roman. "Our realm is not for humans to harvesting dark water. You must leave."

While still kneeling, Roman pulls a syringe from his pocket, jams the needle into the water, and takes some liquid evil into his injection. As he does this, Roman speaks to one of his warriors. "This syringe already has an elixir inside—it's magic of my own design. Now we need to see if it interacts with the dark water." Roman shakes the syringe. The liquid in the injection side glows purple. Roman beams. "It worked."

Lady Aurelian raises her scepter. "You like magic?

Leave now or you'll see some battle spells. I don't wish to hurt lesser beings, but I will."

Roman focuses on the queen. "You don't understand. Americans have invaded my homeland. We have no time." Roman marches across the green and jams the syringe into the neck of the nearest soldier. The man crumples over in pain. When the warrior stands again, he's pale a death. Long fangs now descend from his mouth.

This man is the first Audax.

"See?" Roman gestures to the new vampire. "Behold the unbeatable super solider. One warrior isn't enough, clearly. I need more water so I can make a mighty army. Show us to your nearest lake. Bring us barrels as well."

Lady Aurelian glares at Roman. "You do not give orders here."

"I disagree. Take me now. Refuse me, and I'll just return when the connection between our worlds opens once more."

Lady Aurelian narrows her eyes. "You don't know *how* to come back."

"Fifteen years from now. The ides of March. Midnight. Just past the golden temple. See? I know how to return. Now show me to your nearest lake. I've no time for this."

My heart beats at double speed. Roman just blabbed

how we can return to El Dorado, only not in a simulation. For real!

Sure, the Ides of March is only days away. But why get picky? Maybe we have years before the gateway opens again.

But Roman said the Germans were about to lose World War II. I make some quick calculations. My stomach sinks. We don't have years until the gateway opens again. We definitely have days. Yipes.

Lady Aurelian slams her scepter onto the ground. Fresh concentric circles ripple over the earth. This time, the golden waves pull Roman and his buddies back into the cave. Seconds later, the skull-like mouth slams shut.

A flash of white light appears beside us. When the brightness dies down, Nostra Quattro stands nearby. At least I think it's the same guy. Now it's a young hottie who wears Nostra Quattro's robes.

"I promised you two simulations and one battle," announces Nostra Quattro. "Your first one was a journey into the past. This second will be a creation from my own imagination, although you will learn insights along the way. Get ready for battle."

Another flash of white light follows. When this round of brightness ends, Mack and I now stand in a darkened basement. Nostra Quattro is gone.

A pair of figures steps into the chamber. One is the

old-guy version of Roman. The other is a young kid I don't recognize.

"Cole," whispers Mack.

"Who?"

"He's one of my Zoetic."

Roman stalks up to Mack. "You're such a fool, my boy."

"Is Roman supposed to see us?" I ask. "The other people couldn't tell we were around."

"If they're part of the battle simulation, then they can always detect us." Mack pulls his dagger out from its holster. I arc my tail over my shoulder.

Battle time against Roman. This makes me a happy dragon.

"Oh, Mack." Roman makes an annoying tsk-tsk noise. "You have no idea who you really are and what you can do."

Since Mack is glaring at Roman, I step around Cole. The kid looks normal enough. Then I see it—a monster unlike anything I've ever encountered. It now lurks before me under the illusion of being human.

I don't need any introductions. Without question, this is a Toxicant.

"Come on out, buddy," I declare. "If you're going to fight, let's see you."

The illusion of Cole melts away. Instead, there's a

blue-skinned demon with a mouth of blackened fangs. No doubt, those teeth are dripping with poison.

Mack points to the Toxicant while still glaring at Roman. "What have you done?"

"Every fifteen years, I tried to return to El Dorado and get more black water. Lady Aurelian turned me away every time. But when the gateway opens this year? The queen won't be able to stop me. I'll get all the dark water I need." Roman nods toward the Toxicant. "What you see here is a test. A proof of concept, as we scientists say. I saved enough dark water to see what I can do. Now try to fight him."

Roman lifts his arm. A scepter of his own appears in his right hand. Roman slams the staff onto the floor. Purple light bursts around the guy. A moment later, Roman is gone.

And the Toxicant lunges right for us.

TOXICANT

14

KAPS

*F*ast as a whip, the Toxicant scales up the wall, does a somersault, and lands on my freaking back. The thing has pokey fingers that dig into my skin.

Not okay.

Here is where I run into what you one might call a limitation of my confinement. To escape my tower, I can't take along any metal. So I don't have my handy golden stakes with me tonight.

Good thing Mack came prepared. My guy pulls out a stake from a holster on his thigh.

I'm too busy to ask him to share, though. The Toxicant on my back has gotten busy. The monster grips my head with his left hand and my shoulder with his right. Then the vampire tries to rip me in two. At least, it feels that way. What the Toxicant really wants to do is to chomp my neck with his poisoned teeth.

Not a fan of this idea.

Rushing backward, I slam my back against the wall, crushing the monster against the concrete. For its part, my tail wraps around the Toxicant's ankle and drags it down and away from my throat.

Clever tail.

The rhana magic within me comes to life once more. I can see Mack is if he's sheathed in gold. My own body looks like it's surrounded in fire. Trajectories align. Plans appear. All of a sudden, I know exactly how Mack and I can work together to take down this monster. The only question is when.

"Now!" cries Mack.

I don't need to be told twice. Just as I saw through our rhana bond, I crouch low. Mack leaps forward. In one swift move, my guy stabs the Toxicant right through the chest with a golden stake. The monster howls before crumbling away into dust.

A final flare of white light surrounds us. This time, the brightness takes us back to the grounds behind the Fortress. Mack pats me down from head to toe. "Are you all right?"

"Fine. You might need to check my ass again though, just to be sure."

Mack chuckles. "Only you, Kaps." He gives me a little swat on the butt, which I very much appreciate.

I exhale. "Is it really over now?"

"It is, only I wish it weren't," says Mack. "We could use another round of simulations. The information we just discovered is key." He cups his hand by his mouth. "Nostra Quattro? We need another spell."

I pat my pocket. "And I have more enchanted goodies here." *Which is true.* A girl needs to be prepared.

Long minutes tick by with no response from Nostra Quattro. I frown. "Maybe we should have waited to give him the wrist cuff until later. He's probably off on his honeymoon by now."

"True." Mack shakes his head. "Even so, that was one amazing simulation. At last, we know when and where the doors to El Dorado will open."

"There are other things about that journey which still bug me."

"Like what?"

"You resembled one of those Wyverns. Vasiliás IX. And when Roman spoke the name Lucas, you looked like you might fall over."

Mack bobs his head, considering. "I do have a little bit of demon DNA. Maybe I'm part Wyvern. From what we saw in the simulation of their past, it looks like Wyverns mate with humans."

"There's more."

Mack grins. "Lay in on me."

I point right at his face. "You look healthier now. Not that you looked terrible before, but…" I leave the thought out there.

"I get what you mean." Mack takes in a long breath. "I do feel much better."

"Great G says it's our family gift/curse to constantly be saving the world. She and grandpa Lincoln have a blast doing it."

Mack nods. "I can't help but feel as if something big is coming. But do you know what's crazy? I don't feel drained anymore. I'm looking forward to it."

I jam my hands in my pockets. For some reason, this next bit makes me feel shy. "It could be our rhana bond, you know."

Mack steps nearer. "You may not believe this, but back when we were fighting the Toxicant? I saw you as encircled in red flame."

I smile my face off. "And I saw you in golden fire."

In this moment, I want to tell Mack so many things. How our rhana magic makes my soul sing… that I think we make great partners… and how love really can conquer all.

But my logical side slams down on all that. Mack and

I have some huge strikes against us. Some rhana magic can't make that disappear.

Mack closes the distance between us. Leaning in, he pauses right when his mouth is above mine. Desire pulses through my core. I go up on tiptoe, ready to press my lips to his.

A voice echoes through the night. "Excusez-moi?"

I take a mega-step away from Mack. "Gage?" I ask. "Is that you?"

It's true that I've seen Gage smooch Huntress a number of times. All of which is why I want to keep my own kisses private.

Sure enough, Gage steps out of the shadows. "Bien sur. Mack asked me to inform you both when your hour is up. This kind fellow showed me where to find you."

Another figure moves to stand beside Gage. It's Cole. Mack rushes up to the boy.

"Cole! Are you all right?"

"I'm fine," says Cole. "I've been hanging out with Gage."

I step around Cole in a slow circle. After our experience in the training simulation, I now know how to spot both an Audax and a Toxicant.

"The kid is clean," I announce.

"Of course, I am." Cole hugs his elbows. "What's this about?"

"Nothing." Mack gives Cole a friendly pat on the shoulder. "Kaps and I are little off after our battle simulation, that's all."

Gage clears his throat. "You may thank me now for helping you."

Mack rolls his eyes. "I didn't ask you to babysit me and Kaps."

"Let me put it this way," says Gage. "If you two start kissing, then Princess Kaps will be late. And if that happens, then the imperials may discover who helped her escape. That would not work well for me. I like the current situation. It's the only time I get to almost die at the hands of the woman I love."

Which makes total sense. And we are running short on time. I glance over to Mack. "Next Saturday?"

He winks. "Next Saturday."

With that, I change into my dragon form and take to the skies. Far below me, Mack, Cole and Gage become small specks on the ground. Thankfully I have enough time to fly to the portal instead of relying on my escape ring to transport me there. After all, nothing is better than feeling the Earth's wind on your scales.

Such a beautiful night.

15

KAPS
SUNDAY

Battle simulations with Mack are a blast. But guess what's *almost* as enjoyable? Waking up the next morning. Instead of moping around, I find myself in a super-awesome mood.

And I get to see Mack again next Saturday.

Rolling over, I spy a familiar sight across the room. Huntress sits in her favorite chair while staring out the window. Not sure how she does it. The metal of that seat is so cold, I can't wear shorts on it or I worry my thighs will stick.

Still, it's Huntress' fave spot. Guess the cold suits her mood.

"Good morning, Huntress."

Long seconds tick by before my sister speaks.

"You snuck out," she announces.

"And I came back. Don't forget that part."

"Gage was behind this," Huntress says in a monotone. "He slipped you an escape ring. With that and the band I made, you were able to fly out of Furonium undetected."

"Maybe you can say that a little louder. I don't think every guard in the tower heard you."

Huntress sighs. "I placed a privacy ward on this room. What we say here stays a secret."

Which means it's time for a little game I like to call, *find the hidden privacy ward.* I scan my bedroom, once.

Twice.

Then I see it.

"The dead spider in the corner," I announce. "That's actually fake and loaded with magic."

The slightest smile quirks one side of Huntress' mouth, but the grin vanishes pretty quickly. "I know how you hate spiders."

And there she goes, speaking in that odd monotone again. It's like living with a computer from a human parking garage.

"Everyone hates spiders," I add. "That's why it is indeed the perfect ward."

Huntress lets out another sigh. "Gage gave you contraband and I said nothing. He's a criminal and I'm allowing him to visit and place your life at risk. I keep breaking my vows as Enforcer."

I slip on a robe. "Last night, Mack and I get some key clues that could save humanity from a new breed of vampire. Does it help to know that?"

"Never."

"Okay, then." *Not a lot of gray area when it comes to the mind of Huntress.*

For the first time, I notice something gripped in my sister's hands. I cross the room and read over her shoulder because that's how I roll. Turns out, it's an invitation.

You are cordially invited to a guided tour of the Hexenwing Relic Museum

After that, there's a lot of nonsense about what to wear and the fact that people who are locked in towers shouldn't attend. Whatever. If I were a cartoon character, I'd have stars coming out of my head right now.

Relic hunting is my thing.

After all, let's not forget that I have a whole hidden lair dedicated to storing all my magical stuff. A girl has to keep her inventory fresh.

I round on Huntress. "The Hexenwing Relic Museum? That dragon tribe specializes in magic."

"I know."

"And now I know that you know. or something."

"The Hexenwings sent too many invitations. It's suspicious."

Okay, Huntress may have another point there, but it's a small one when compared to the massive opportunity for new treasure. "When were you going to tell me about this?"

"Never," says Huntress. "As I explained before, no matter how many times I refuse, the Hexenwings keep sending me invitations. It's strange." She sighs for a third time. "We aren't going. Besides, you know how Mistress Cerys is when it comes to you."

Sadly, Huntress is spot on the money once more. To me, Mistress Cerys is like that borderline-creepy instructor who makes you sit in the front row as teacher's pet… when you'd rather hide or barf on her shoes. Whenever I see Cerys, she gets a vision about me in five minutes, tops. And these prophecies are all annoying, personal, and told at top volume to a room full of strangers. Or worse, she insists she has to visit me at home for a more accurate reading. Those sessions are even worse.

"You shouldn't go on this tour," continues Huntress.

I sniff. "I shouldn't do a lot of things. But this is treasure we're talking about here. I can handle it."

"I disagree." Huntress starts shuffling her way toward the door.

A memory appears. "Mistress Cerys had a vision about you once."

Huntress pauses on the threshold. "When?"

"You were four years old."

Huntress frowns. "How would you remember this?"

"Because it was so exceptional for Cerys to pick on you for a change. I remember exactly what she said." Here I spread out my arms for dramatic effect, which is a key part of any Cerys impression. *I see her future. Ogres will bring Huntress freedom.*"

"That was the worst prediction ever. I've never even met an ogre." With that, Huntress slumps her way out of the room.

For a long minute, I debate recruiting some performing mimes to cheer my sister up, then dismiss the idea. Knowing Huntress, she might end up fighting them.

Setting aside my Happy Huntress Program, I refocus on the best topic in all of Furonium. *Relics.*

Pacing my room, I picture the best way to slip out of the tower for Cerys' tour. Mind you, this isn't as tricky as leaving the entire realm, but it still needs some scheming.

And I'm just the girl to make it happen.

16

KAPS

FRIDAY

8:38 AM

After five long days of waiting, I finally stand inside the famous Relic Museum of the Hexenwing dragons. The place looks like a combination of an Old West Boudoir and a black marble mausoleum. In other words, there's a lot of dark stone, bright red velvet, and gilded everything. What can I say? The Hexenwings love magic and drama.

For my part, I love treasure. Hence why I'm here today. And in case you're wondering, Huntress hasn't exactly approved this visit. But I snuck out anyway because TREASURE.

That said, I'm not a dumbass. There's no need to announce my presence. All of which is why I take care to hang back from the main group of tour goers.

Considering all the dark walls and shadowy alcoves in this place, hiding is not a problem.

At the opposite side of the passage, Cerys leads about thirty dragon shifters on her tour. For her part, Cerys tall and lanky woman who wears a fitted sheath of black silk. A long headdress of black peacock feathers cascades down her back.

Directly behind Cerys are my sisters, Huntress and Zin. Neither of them know I'm here because if they did, what's the fun in that?

So far, Cerys has spent an hour going through wall displays on the history of relic seeking. Not one bit of treasure to be seen. I'm starting to get anxious.

Cerys pauses before a stretch of wall that holds yet another embedded display case. Beyond the glass panel sits all sorts of sparkly stuff.

At last. Treasure.

My tail sways behind me in a chipper rhythm while a lot of words tumble out of Cerys' mouth. All I catch are blah blah blah super valuable *blah blah blah* don't touch *blah blah blah.*

At this point, it would be way smarter to stay behind the crowd. But I can't see crap that way, so I slowly steal up toward the display case.

It's a good move.

Beyond the glass pane, I see a bunch of dusty skulls—

which is gross—but also a lovely and glittering wizard's staff. Someone took care to remove all the cobwebs from this golden thing.

That person is my new best friend.

The scepter itself is simply glorious. I'm talking five feet high, made of gold, and with an obvious stone of magic perched on top. Modern wizards just don't make cool stuff like this anymore. Even better, this relic is from a Wyvern.

Suddenly, someone taps the glass while speaking in an overly loud voice. "Where did you find that staff?"

With a gasp, I realize that mystery speaker was me. *Oops.* I have great impulse control… until I don't. Story of my life.

Cerys' mouth grinds out silent words for three full seconds before she finds her voice. "Princess Kaps, is that you? Wait everyone, I'm starting to get a vision!"

At this point, there could be flashing lights over Cerys' head and an announcer saying, *danger, danger!* I simply must stop this situation from going off the rails. If my parents find out I escaped again, things could get awkward.

Correction. *Awkward-er.*

This isn't my first time getting in trouble. I have a wide array of options on hand for just such occasions. "Excuse me, Mistress Cerys?"

She opens her right eye. "I'm trying to get a vision."

"Don't you want to do that later, though? Maybe at my tower or something? You'll get a much better read that way."

Cerys opens both eyes now. "Why would I do that?"

"Because you've been standing there for twenty minutes." *Total lie.*

Cerys gasps. "Is that true?"

"I don't know," I deadpan. "Is it?"

At this point, I shoot sly look toward Huntress, but she's staring at the floor in misery. No response. So I turn to Zinnia instead. Zin is my identical twin, only her hair is white-blonde and in dreads. A small smile rounds her mouth. She's totally enjoying this.

"That is the truth," declares Zin. "Please continue with the tour."

Cerys shifts her weight from foot to foot. "I'm not sure."

"Perhaps I can sing and entertain everyone while you decide?" asks Zin.

At this news, the crowd bursts into happy chatter. Zin is an amazing musician; everyone wants to hear her. Meanwhile, Cerys is a bit of an attention hog. Zin's offer gets the Mistress Dragon moving and how.

"I appreciate the idea," says Cerys. "But we shall continue on our tour now."

Zin and I share a fist bump as the group walks away. Once everyone is well and out of dight, I return my attention to my favorite display case. Reaching into my jacket pocket, I take out my handy—and totally enchanted—pink eraser. This is a trick I learned from my grandpa Lincoln, by the way. When you're carrying around magic, it's best to make it look like a regular object.

I set the magic eraser against the glass. "Awaken and get me that scepter."

Sure enough, the object shimmies its way through the glass pane. Once inside, it hops from the top of one skull to the next. I should have known this was bum magic. The witch I bought it from was a total kook.

"Stop goofing around," I warn. "The scepter."

The eraser mope-bounces over to the staff. Once it reaches the end, the pink object stretches to encompass the entire scepter, then it shrinks back to eraser size.

"Perfect," I whisper. "Now get back here."

The eraser slinks back to the glass and pops through to the other side. "Thank you," I state. "Please go back to sleep." The eraser returns to being a regular object once more.

I slip my magical find into my pocket and feel mighty good about my bad self.

Suddenly, a creeping sensation moves up my neck.

I'm being watched. Twisting about, I scan the hallway. The place is deserted. How long have I been standing here by this case? Long enough to become a target, that's for sure.

At this point, I could think that I'm just imagining things. But I've faced down dozens of vampires. My inner dragon senses when a predator is near. There's no mistaking the sensation.

Someone's about to attack.

17

KAPS

My dragon's sense starts to go berserk. *Predator!* It seems to scream. *Beware!* I step around in a slow circle, on alert for any sign of danger.

The lights flicker and darken. Adrenaline kicks through my system. My thoughts circle back to my battle training with Mack. This is what happened when the faked-up Toxicant attacked. The lights went out first.

I pat my pockets. I brought some relics, but nothing that would help against a Toxicant. True, I just picked up a cool wand. But it's unclear what—if anything—that scepter can do.

Leaning down, I check the holster at my ankle. Sure, I know that I've been leaving metal stuff behind since it sets off the tower's alarms, but maybe I just got lucky and it's still there.

But the holster is empty.

Okay, I can improvise.

With gentle movements, I pull down a near picture from the wall and snap off one side of the frame. Sure enough, the frame is gilded. That's just a paper-thin coating of gold, but it should be enough.

With my makeshift weapon in hand, I can do one of two things. The first is run for my life. Not an option. If there really is an Audax—or worse, a Toxicant—then running just gives them an easy target. As in, my back.

And why flee when I'm so very good in battle?

I carefully scan the shadowy passage. Once again, I lean into my memories from the battle simulation with Mack. We'd somehow connected with each other. *Rhana magic.* It was natural enough to do when we were side by side, but could it work across a distance?

One way to find out.

I picture Mack and the golden glow that appeared over his skin. Suddenly, a rush of energy moves through me. I smile from ear to ear.

Yes. I've tapped in.

With my new power behind me, I inspect the hallway once more. At first, I see nothing. Then a thin layer of golden fire surrounds a distant figure.

More rhana magic.

This time, my connection to Mack reveals how one of the Cerys' guards lurks near the wall. I scan the figure more carefully.

Hold on. That's not a guard. It's a Toxicant.

The true look of this souped-up vampire matches what I saw in the battle simulation. This new Toxicant sports blue skin, pointy fingers and gangly limbs. Oh, and let's not forget my favorite part: all those long fangs that drip venom.

As I've learned over the years, not all Audax have the same strengths in battle. I'm guessing the same is true for Toxicants. This one isn't rushing into a fight, which works for me. I can size up my opponent.

Time to chat up the vampire.

I tighten my grip on my stake. "I see you."

"That's not possible."

"You're not Audax. You're Toxicant. And you're standing by the statue of Mistress Cerys. Now *you* tell *me* what's possible."

The Toxicant pauses. There's the tell-tale intake of breath that means he hears me and isn't happy.

Good.

I slip down the hallway. The Toxicant tilts his head, but doesn't track my movement across the passage.

Which means that while I can see him, the Toxicant can't see me as easily.

Even better.

I sneak even closer to my target. Once more, the Toxicant doesn't seem to notice my movement. I raise my stake to shoulder-height and get ready to pounce. Just a few more yards, then I'll be close enough to attack.

The Toxicant tilts back his head and sniffs the air. After that, everything happens so quickly, it's hard to keep track. The Toxicant leaps in my direction and lands squarely on my chest. I'm knocked back-first onto the chilly marble floor.

Turns out, this particular Toxicant has an exceptional sense of smell combined with crappy night vision.

Now I know.

Fast as a whip, the thing sinks its teeth into my shoulder.

Pain spikes down my arm. Something inside me screams in terror and pain. The Toxicant wraps his chilly hands around my throat.

"I just killed your dragon. Now I'll end you."

At last, my mind and body catch up with the fast pace of events. Biting me was the Toxicant's big mistake. It should have just taken me down while it had an opening. Now I can counter-attack.

The creature's grip is so tight, it feels as if my throat's

being crushed. My lungs scream for air. Even so, I'm not missing this chance.

At my command, my tail whips up. The arrowhead-shaped end wraps around the base of my homemade stake. Then it swoops the weapon up into the air and slams it into the Toxicant's back. The monster screams as it bursts into a cloud of particles.

Now that's what I call dead.

I turn away while closing my eyes tightly. No way do I want to breathe in a lungful of mutant monster dust.

The lights flicker back on. I scooch away from what remains of the vampire, all while sucking in lungfuls of lovely air. I brush at my shoulder as the gravity of things settles in.

Killed my dragon? Not possible. My tail is still around.

All I need to do is shift forms a little bit. That will prove the Toxicant is a lying liar. I imagine my arms being covered in dragon scales. Nothing happens. Next I picture a full transformation into my dragon form. Still, zero happens.

A voice echoes into the hallway. "Kaps?"

I exhale. "Over here, Huntress."

Huntress steps into the passageway. "There are strange folks meandering around here. For a minute, I even thought I saw Mum and Da." She stops cold. "What happened?" She jogs over to kneel at my side. "Something bit you."

"A Toxicant. It took away my ability to shift."

"A what?"

"Toxicant. It's an advanced kind of Audax."

"You mean those vampires you kill? What would they be doing here in Furonium?"

"Huntress." I shoot her a dry look. "My boyfriend runs a secret league that kills these monsters. From a strategic point of view, it makes sense that they'd want to kill both me and my inner dragon."

"And you're sure you can't shift?"

"Not right now." I force on a smile. "But who knows? I have a secret lair that's packed with magical relics. Maybe there's some way to fix this."

"And I was going to get on your case about stealing that scepter." Huntress wraps her arm around my shoulder. "Are you all right to walk? We must get to your lair."

"That can wait. What about Cerys?"

"Zin is giving an impromptu concert. No one will notice us leaving."

"No, I mean the Toxicant took on the appearance of a Hexenwing guard. We need to warn everyone."

"And that's best to do from the palace, which is where your lair is hidden. It will also give us cover for why you're with me. Officially, you're staying in the dungeon."

I can't help but grin. "You're always right, Huntress. It's a little annoying."

She chuckles. "Call it a gift."

"Let's go." I haul myself to stand. Unfortunately, the entire right-hand side of my body feels numb. Whatever this poison is, it's heavy-duty stuff.

"You can't fly to the palace, can you?" asks Huntress.

"No, but I have a little gift from Gage that will help." I show off my new bling. "With these rings, we can transport directly into my lair. Just wrap your arm over my shoulder. That way, the magic will see us as one person.

Huntress does as requested. Within a few minutes, my sister and I are standing in my lair. As always, the place is a massive cavern lined with shelves, drawers, books and magical awesomeness.

I step over to a box of vials and start sorting through the ones that might prove helpful. I motion to Huntress. "Separate these into light and dark elixirs for me, will you?"

While Huntress moves the little bottles around, I pull out cauldrons and mix the potions together in about a dozen different ways. Eventually, I've downed as much elixir as I can handle without barfing. And while I finish chugging the last of my foul-tasting goop, Huntress gets messages out to everyone.

If it all works out, then my dragon-self will return within forty-eight hours.

I can only wait and see.

18

MACK

SATURDAY

1 1:58 PM.

Almost time.

I pace a line on the Fortress grounds. Ever since last night, I've felt nervous energy zinging through me. With every passing hour, I can sense more of Kaps through our rhana bond.

Something is wrong.

A few yards away, a point of white light appears at eye-level in the darkness. The spot of brightness swirls larger until it's a circle that looms six feet high.

Kaps steps through.

She wears her boots, leather pants and a fitted dark top. Normally, I'd take a moment to soak in her beauty. This time, I'm too distracted.

Kaps loves to fly in her dragon form. Now that she

has both an escape ring and a replicator band, Kaps should be able to just pass through the portal to Earth and wing her way over here. Why is she walking straight through?

A thread of worry twists inside me. This has something to do with the trouble I've sensed through our bond since last night. Crossing the Fortress grounds, I wrap my woman in a warm embrace. That's when it hits me.

Something is wrong with Kaps' scent.

I break our hug. "What happened?"

"I took down a Toxicant last night. It bit me. Now I can't shift."

I cup her face in my hands. "Are you worried?"

"My lair is crammed with magical relics. Something in there should fix this problem. I took a bunch of potions last night."

I know my woman. She's still concerned. "And?"

"Nothing's working yet." Kaps leans into my embrace and I gently stroke her hair. "I hate this," whispers Kaps. "I want my dragon back."

A mixture of guilt and rage battle it out inside me "This is my fault. If you weren't connected to me, Roman would never have sent a Toxicant after you."

"Come on. It's not like I didn't kill Roman's minions

for years. The man has plenty of reasons to take me down."

It's tempting to just accept what Kaps says and move on. But I can't. It feels dishonest.

"Roman never went after you before we got mixed up together."

We share a long gaze. I can tell what Kaps is thinking, because the same thought churns through my mind.

This relationship is impossible.

After a while, the silence becomes unbearable.

"Are you still up for battle simulation?" I ask. "I have another enchanted sword from Nostra Quattro. The wizard himself is still missing, so it'll just be standard practice."

"I brought something else." Kaps reaches into her pocket and pulls out what looks like a small eraser. "Wake up," she whispers to the magical item. The eraser lengthens and transforms into something new.

A golden scepter.

I let out a low whistle. This isn't a modern-style Nostra Quattro special. Even when the wizard enchants a sword, it's a rather simple blade. This scepter weaves together different strands of gold into a long mural of dragons. A prickle of awareness runs over my skin.

Not dragons.

Wyverns.

Stepping forward, I hold out my hands, palms upward. "May I see it?"

"Sure." Kaps sets the staff onto my bare skin. A thrill of power moves up my arms.

"Wow," I say, my voice husky. "This thing is loaded with magic."

Kaps gestures along the length of the scepter. "This motif has these cords which connect one Wyvern to another. I think it's used for communication spells."

I brush my fingers across the intricate metalwork. "It won't be easy to connect with any Wyverns. They're all locked off in another dimension."

"True." Kaps bobs her brows. "Seems like it's worth a try, though. Am I right or am I right?"

"So right." I move to hand the scepter back to Kaps. "Give it a go."

"Thanks, but no thanks." A serious look tightens across Kaps' face. "I think you should do it."

"Why?"

"When I fought the Toxicant last night, I leaned into our rhana bond."

"And I felt the pull. Afterward, I sensed your sorrow. I didn't know you'd lost your dragon, though."

"The only reason I was able to take down the Toxicant was because our rhana magic helped me see that monster in the dark. The Toxicant appeared to be surrounded in a thin layer of golden fire." She scans me from head to toe and sighs. "That's how you look right now. It started the moment you clasped that scepter. You should use the staff, Mack. I think that's what the bond wants us to do." She winces. "That probably sounds unhinged."

I clasp the scepter more tightly. Words pour from me. I've never consciously thought this before, but the moment I speak the idea aloud, I know it's true.

"You're anything but unhinged," I declare. "The way we were both drawn toward fighting Audax and obsessing about Wyverns… I believe our rhana bond has been pulling strings on us for years. Now we're just getting better at sensing what the magic desires."

Kaps smiles. "In that case, do the thing with the thing. Let's see what happens."

I lift the scepter, ready to slam it on the ground. Then I pause. "Magic works best if I picture what I want it to do. Any suggestions?

"There was that bust in El Dorado who looked like you. Imagine that guy's face."

I nod. "Whatever bit of demonic DNA I have, it must have some Wyvern in it. I think that will activate the magic perfectly."

Picturing the man from El Dorado, I slam the scepter onto the ground. Round golden waves roll out from the spot. The colored light speeds through the trees that surround the Fortress green. A moment later, a figure steps out from the shadows. Every cell in my body seems to freeze.

It's Lady Aurelian.

As she moves closer, I realize it's a semi-transparent version of Lady Aurelian. This is indeed another communication spell.

And it's working.

Lady Aurelian raises her arm, palm forward. It's a universal gesture for, *give me a second.*

Kaps and I exchange a long look. Shock and excitement zing between us.

Lady Aurelian. This is really happening. The Wyvern queen is here in her human form. Or at least, in a colorful and semi-transparent version. Still, she appears as elegant as she did in Nostra Quattro's simulation.

A few yards away, Lady Aurelian lowers her hand. "I am ready now, although my time is limited."

I pull Kaps to my side. "I'm Mack. This is Kaps."

A smile quicks her mouth. "I know who you are, just as you know me. Or, at least you *think* you do." The queen gestures toward the scepter in my hand. "What you hold is a Wyvern wand of summoning. It found me and said you wished to connect. But I still need to meet the magic and send you my signal." She lowers her head. "That part isn't easy."

"Do you need any help?" I ask. "I have healing magic back at the Fortress."

"No," answers Lady Aurelian. "There isn't time for such things. And I'd have given up much more of my energy for the chance to see you face to face." Lady Aurelian scans me with a strange look.

"Is something wrong?" I ask.

"Quite the contrary. You've grown up so well, my son."

The word hits me like a punch to the gut. *Son.*

Kaps gently sets her hand on my arm. With her touch, the rhana bond between us kicks into action. Golden light appears around me once more. And with that power comes absolute certainty.

I am the child of Lady Aurelian.

LADY AURELIAN

19

MACK

The word ricochets through me in strange ways. *My son.* Suddenly, so many odd circumstances make perfect sense. There's the way Kaps and I are such strong rhanas even though I'm supposedly human with just a little demon DNA.

That was all a lie. We're rhanas because I'm a Wyvern and Kaps is a dragon. We are both born to form a mate bond.

And then, there's the way Kaps and I love Wyvern lore. Only a rhana bond with tons of power behind it could drive such an obsession.

Not to mention the voice that's always been calling to me from the shadows.

My eyes widen. "That was you, wasn't it?" I ask. "You were the one whispering to me all those years."

"Yes," answers Mother. "It was me." The color in her transparent form begins to fade. Her magic is running out. "You must have many questions," she adds. "Allow me to tell you what I can in the little time that remains. I have prepared many years for this moment."

I nod. "Of course."

"You are the grandson of Vasiliás IX, the greatest king of the Wyverns and my beloved father." When she says the next part, her voice breaks. "You look just like him."

A weight of grief presses in around me. At the same time, I'm filled with so much joy, my body feels weightless. Roman raised me that I was left on the doorstep to the Zoetic Fortress without any note or explanation. And that was all another lie. I have a family and history.

Somehow, I'm able to force out a single question. "What is my name?"

"Macaidan. You are my son and only heir."

Kaps leans her head against my shoulder. I wrap my arm around her waist. In the torrent of emotions around me, she's my rock.

Lady Aurelian sighs. "To save our people, I transported us to a different existence. There remains a portal that connects Earth to El Dorado. We call it the Divide. But once you step through that entryway, you do not come directly to our realm. Instead, you enter the cave that imprisons two demon-titans, Vision and the Darkness."

I open my mouth, ready to explain that I saw much of this in my simulation from Nostra Quattro. But my mother spent many years planning out these words. I want to hear them as she wished them to be shared. So I listen.

"Some activate the portal, enter the caverns, and are never seen again," continues mother. "Still, once every fifteen years, my magic sends Vision and the Darkness into an enchanted sleep. It only lasts for an hour, but that time is enough for some humans—ones who again have felt the pull of my spell—to step through the cavern unharmed. They walk out again via what we call the Fangs. Once there, the newcomers are greeted by Wyverns and given a choice. We quickly explain where they are and give them a chance to return to the human world."

Chills run up my arm as I picture the dark cavern with its horrible demon-titans. After that, how marvelous would it be to step out of the shadows and into a welcome party of Wyverns? Suddenly, the desire to see my own people burns through me so strongly, it's as if my entire body were on fire.

"And do any humans return to Earth?" asks Kaps.

"Only Roman and his men," answers Mother. "And

that was because I drove him away." She wobbles from foot to foot. No question about it.

We don't have long before her strength runs out.

"The first time Roman came though, he took dark water—the very foul liquid that runs through our land. Roman used its power to create the first Audax. Once it became clear what Roman *really* wanted, I drove him away. But every fifteen years, Roman walks through the gateway to our world. Each time he returns, he's stronger. And thanks to the dark magic poisoning our land, I grew weaker."

Mother's eyes shimmer with tears. "You were four years old when Roman stole you away from me. He injected you with poison that removed your inner Wyvern."

Beside me, Kaps stiffens. I've never shown so much as a scale, let alone shift into Wyvern form. And now Roman has given the same venom to Kaps. That's not good news for her dragon.

"I'm sorry, my son." Mother shakes her head. "I've done what I could to preserve the Wyverns. I'm the last royal and I have failed. Vision and the Darkness still imprison our people. Every year, the dark water takes more lives and our numbers dwindle. Now, my power is all but gone. Roman knows I cannot hold him off again."

"I can't allow that," I declare. "There must be something I can do."

"On the Ides of March, you must enter our realm, take my place as ruler and—most important of all—kill Roman."

To do that, I must become separated from everyone I know. Forever. Still, I can't refuse her or my people. "I understand."

"Your people need you, son. Once Roman is gone, there will be nothing to keep you on Earth. Zoetic have no purpose without Audax and Toxicants… And I have waited too long to hold my child again."

With that, her ghostly form vanishes. Silence presses in around us. Kaps is the first to speak.

"You must go to El Dorado and kill Roman."

"Yes."

"The door stays open for an hour. I'll help you as long as I can."

I round on Kaps. "Promise you won't do that. You can't shift. I'm weak enough as it is. If I'm worrying about you, I'll be useless."

Kaps' lower lip wobbles. "Then I won't see you again for fifteen years."

How it kills me to say this.

"No, you won't see me again, ever. Mother is right. With Roman gone, there's no place for me on Earth.

And you need to find a rhana bond with another dragon. Live out a life where your parents can join. And someday, maybe you'll have little dragonlings who play with your sisters' children. That's what I want for you. It's what you *deserve*."

"I want to stay in El Dorado, but I can't only see my family once every fifteen years."

"And I'd never ask that of you." I kiss her forehead softly and step away. "It's time to go."

Kaps' pocket buzzes. She pulls out her cell phone and checks the screen. "It's Huntress. Mistress Cerys wants to see me at the tower immediately. She has a vision."

"That's a sign," I declare. "Leave me."

Kaps nods. A moment later, a round portal of white magic appears. Kaps steps through it and out of my life.

Forever.

20

KAPS

I walk out of the portal and into a secluded hallway of my tower.

No one's here. Nice.

I soon make my way into the reception hall proper. It's a massive space with arched ceilings. Tapestries line the walls, one for each major dragon tribe. At the far end of the hall are a pair of tall thrones. Mum is on the red one. Like always, she looks regal with her petite frame, white-blonde hair and piercing eyes. Beside her sits Da. He's all dark coloring and hefty muscles. I try reading their expressions, but they reveal nothing in their faces.

One detail does say a lot, though. Mum wears a red gown while Da sports a dark military uniform. Regal outfits mean official business.

Am I in trouble?

I scan the room. Mistress Cerys isn't here. My sisters stand nearby. Huntress sports her purple battle leathers while Zin is dressed in jeans and a big sweater.

Another figure comes into view. This one lurks in the shadows behind the throne.

A Toxicant.

"Run!" I cry. "That's a vampire."

"We know," says Mum. "And you're an expert at destroying his kind."

I freeze. Since when do my parents acknowledge my secret life as a vampire killer?

I wince. "Mistress Cerys isn't coming here, is she?"

"No," replies Mum.

"And where did you get that Toxicant?" I ask.

"This fellow tried to break into the tower," explains Da. "He made the mistake of drinking some gold-infused wine. Once the magic reaches his heart, he'll be gone."

My brows lift. Magical wine infused with gold… that's a great way to kill both Audax and Toxicants. Why hadn't I thought of that before?

Mum glances over her shoulder at the Toxicant. "Come forward, vampire."

The Toxicant stomps out from behind the throne. "I will say nothing."

"That's fine," says Mum. "You already babbled every-thing we need to know." She looks to Da. "How long do you give him?"

Dad purses his lips. "3, 2, 1."

The Toxicant gasps and falls over. His body instantly transforms into a pile of blue ash.

I shake my head. "I'm very confused."

"Come closer and we can talk," says Mum.

I cautiously move nearer to my parents.

"All three of you," adds Da.

My sisters join me in standing before the pair of thrones. Zin clears her throat. "I have something to say."

Mum nods. "Go on."

Zin takes in a deep breath. "Whatever Kaps has done, she's been pulled into it by her rhana bond. Kaps tried to follow her own path while trying to give everyone else the illusion of safety. In her unique way, she acted honorably. I think we should give her a chance to decide how *she* wants to live her life."

Now Zin hasn't always been my greatest supporter. But in this moment?

Best. Sister. Ever.

"We agree," states Da.

My eyes widen. "You do?"

"After what happened at the Zoetic Fortress, Mum

and I knew you'd try to see Mack again. Both of us realize the pull of a rhana bond. And we needed to get some facts straight."

I frown. "I still don't follow."

"Your father and I have been following you," explains Mum.

"Really?" I ask. "Don't you have more important things to do?"

"As a matter of fact, no." Da pierces me with one of his most serious gazes. "Our children are always what's most important. Your history of telling the truth was a little spotty, so your Mum and I decided to take things into our own hands."

"Your own hands." Some part of me knows I'm just repeating what Da says, but that doesn't seem to stop me from doing it.

"We saw you fight that Toxicant in the Hexenwing museum," explains Mum. "You took it down before we even had a chance to intervene."

"Ha," grumbles Huntress. "I knew you two were there."

"We were heartbroken that the creature bit you," adds Da. "But until that moment, we weren't sure these vampires even existed."

"And the situation did give us an opportunity," says

Mum. "We knew another Toxicant would try to attack. That's how we caught this fellow." She gestures to the pile of blue dust on the ground.

"What did you do, exactly?" I ask.

Da shrugs. "We interrogated this fellow over a glass of magical wine. He shared or confirmed what we needed to know."

At this point, things could go one of two ways for me. Very good… or hella badly.

"I can see the question in your eyes," says Mum. "You wonder what we know."

I hold my thumb and pointer finger an inch apart. "Only a little."

"Your rhana is Mack, the rightful King of the Wyverns," says Da. "Are we correct so far?"

I swallow on a suddenly-dry throat. "Oh, yeah."

"Mack will return to El Dorado in a matter of hours," declares Mum. "The city is trapped in another dimension. Access to the Wyvern population is guarded by two demon-titans, Vision and the Darkness. Once there, Mack has sworn to kill Roman and take over ruling his people."

Zin grabs my left arm; Huntress takes the right. "Kaps," says Zin.

"That can't be true," adds huntress.

"It's spot on," I say. "Mum and Da did a really good job." I scan both their faces. Damn, I need to learn how to hide emotions like they do. "What happens next?"

"That depends," says Da. "What do you wish to do?"

I try hard not to sniffle. "Mack and I just talked about it. It's over between us."

My parents share a shocked look. Then they step down from their thrones to stand beside me. "Are you both certain about this?"

I nod.

Mum takes my hands in hers. "Growing up, my family never thought I could do things. They wanted to wrap me up in cotton and keep me safe. It was all because I had a mark on my face that meant I could become a demon someday."

At this point, Mum has my total attention. We've all heard how our mother was supposed to become a Void demon, but she never talks about it.

Mum goes on. "Yet all my life, I had this calling to repair the firmament that holds the after-realms together. Tempest—I mean, your father—believed I could fix everything. He joined me on that mission. Without his love, I wouldn't have survived."

A wistful smile rounds Da's mouth. Like Mum, he's stopped being all regal and turned into a regular father.

"I knew from the moment I saw your mother that she was my fated mate. At the time, she was part human, demon and angel. The bond didn't make any sense. But we trusted in our feelings for each other. In the end, the magic between us transformed your mother into the most powerful dragon in the after-realms."

Mum winks. "It's a tie."

We all chuckle.

Da turns to Zin. "So you see, we have changed our minds."

Mum gives my hands a gentle squeeze. "Know this. I believe in you and your bond to Mack. Whatever decision you make, you have my support."

Da sets his hands atop Mum's. "And mine as well."

"Same here." Zin rests her palms atop the pile.

Huntress hesitates, then stacks her hands on as well. "I don't believe in this rhana stuff, but I do believe in you, Kaps. Whatever you want to do, you'll make it happen."

I take in a deep breath. "I don't know if I can live apart from you all, but I do want to go through the gate to El Dorado. Maybe I can only be there for a few minutes before I have to head back. Still, it will help to know I've done everything I can."

"And would you like company?" asks Da.

"Are you kidding?" I ask. "I'd love it if all whole dragon and angel armies came along."

"You'll have them," says Da.

"Thanks, everyone," I state. "Now let's get to planning. The portal opens in a matter of hours and there's a ton left to do."

21

MACK

*N*didi and I march through a stretch of Amazon jungle. Both of us wear camouflage field gear complete with cargo pants, vest and heavy boots. As we trudge beneath the trees, glimpses of the moon appear through the heavy canopy overhead. The air is thick with humidity. With every breath, I pull in the scent of fresh leaves and stale water.

I grip a magical compass in my right hand. Inside the gold case, a thin metal arrow gyrates under a glass cover. We march along in whatever direction the device dictates.

After hours of stomping through the undergrowth, the arrow on the compass disappears entirely. My breath catches. This is the moment. We've reached the gateway. I pause. Ndidi moves to stand by my side.

Together, my friend and I scan the landscape. We've now stepped away from the heavy canopy and into a marshy clearing.

"Doesn't look like the place to put a portal between realities," says Ndidi. "But I suppose that's the point."

I nod. "Whatever the portal is, it should open any minute now. Lady Aurelian was very specific that the portal was triggered by both place and time."

A thin layer of swampy water covers the ground. Insects dance across the surface, causing small ripples. Off in the darkness, the jungle comes to life. Animals chatter. Birds caw. The Amazon is a noisy place, but this racket is way beyond that. The atmosphere fills with a strong sense of static.

Magic. That's what has everything on edge.

Won't be long now.

The ground rumbles. The swampy water shimmies from the vibrations. The center of the shallow marsh bubbles.

Little by little, a large object ascends from the marsh. It's the gateway to El Dorado—what Lady Aurelian called the Divide. I've spent years researching El Dorado, especially this portal. Some experts pictured it as a glowing door that hovers in the air. Others describe it as a pit that opens in the ground. But it's neither of those. The Divide is a tall circle of stone.

The round structure itself is made from fifteen rock segments, one for each year that must pass before the passageway will open once more. One by one, those segments now flare with blue light. Then all of them darken while the open center of the ring glistens with azure magic.

The Divide is open at last.

THE DIVIDE

22

MACK

The world takes on a dream-like sheen. Before me, the entrance to El Dorado shimmers with light and power. The time has come to move through it.

I'm about to say goodbye to Ndidi when it happens. A high-pitched hum fills the air.

Ndidi and I share a look. There's no missing that particular tone. It's Zoetic transfer magic. We've a machine called the Device which allows teleportation over short distances. It's perfect for moving large groups without anyone being the wiser.

Suddenly, a flare of white light sears across the jungle. The bright blast is painfully intense. When it ends, the high-pitched hum vanishes as well.

Ndidi shakes his head. "If my guess right, Roman just

transported a large group through that portal. Easy enough to do with the Device."

"One way to find out." I slog through the marshy water and pause by the round portal. Close up, the glowing center is semi-transparent.

"What do you see?" asks Ndidi.

"A darkened cave inside," I reply. "There's no one there, however."

"That's typical Roman," says Ndidi. "He plans his missions down to the second. He wouldn't leave people to wait by the portal's interior."

Unease twists through my rib cage. Roman always planned things out excessively… and that with only hours to organize a Zoetic mission. When it comes to El Dorado, Roman's been waiting decades for the Divide to open. He'll have everything coordinated and thought through.

"You don't need me to say this," adds Ndidi. "But stay on your guard for fast attacks that come out of nowhere."

"Agreed. All those years, we thought Roman was just an eccentric inventor who didn't have the patience for a long siege. Now, I see the man was all about Blitzkrieg."

A sour taste rolls up my throat. For so many years, Roman did nothing but lie to me. My muscles tighten with equal measures of rage and helplessness.

Ndidi sets his hand on my shoulder. "There's no time to brood on Roman. Get through the gateway and end this. You'll have years afterward to work everything out. I'll be rooting for you from the Fortress."

A chill of shock prickles over my skin. Growing up, Ndidi and I spent hours playing jungle explorer. Our favorite game was finding the entrance to El Dorado.

Now we're here. *How can I really go on alone?*

"I can see the wheels of your mind turning," says Ndidi. "We talked about this. I'll run the Zoetic. You take charge of those Wyverns." He gives my shoulder a gentle squeeze. "The portal only stays open for an hour, my friend. Whatever you're thinking, it's not the mission. Set it aside."

I can't help but smile. Ndidi always knows what to say. I take in a shaky breath. "I'll miss you."

"And I'll try to miss you, but life promises to be busy."

Ndidi and I discussed his plans. Assuming I get rid of Roman and his vampires, then Ndidi will rebuild the Zoetic as a fighting force for hire. They'll be like Gage and his cronies, only one hundred percent legal.

I nod. "Keep an eye on Kaps for me." Out of all the pain and loss in this day, moving forward without my rhana is the worst devastation of all.

"You know I will."

Turning, I wrap Ndidi in a deep hug. Then I face the portal and step through.

Once I enter the cave, I find a circular and deserted spot. *So far, so good.* At least the interior matches the way it looked from the opposite side of the portal. Now that I'm inside, I do catch more detail. There's one great arched exit from this space. Most likely, that pathway leads to Vision and Darkness. According to Lady Aurelian, those two will sleep for the next hour. I should be able to walk past them in safety.

I take a few steps toward the main passage, then pause. The faint smell of pepper hangs in the air. It could be nothing, or it could be another Zoetic field tool. We use a magical spray to mark trails in the wild. It leaves behind a peppery scent.

Did Roman mark a trail in this cave? It seems odd, considering that there's only one path. Still, it's easy enough to find out the truth. Reaching into a pocket on my cargo vest, I pull out a small penlight. Turning the device on, I cast a little halo of brightness onto the floor.

Sure enough, the light shows a series of rough arrows drawn onto the rock. I follow the markings to what looks like a dark patch on the stone wall. In truth, it's another opening to a smaller passageway.

Huh. Roman must have found a better path through

the caves—one that probably does go past the demon-titans.

But are these marks old or new?

I rub my chin and consider my options. In the end, it doesn't matter if Roman made these marks two minutes or fifteen years ago. It's worth investigating either way. Yet before I do follow the path, I remove my golden spike from its holster.

A man can't be too careful.

Using my small flashlight to guide me, I step through the break in the wall and follow the marks on the floor. The arrows end by pointing toward what appears to be a solid sheet of stone.

Was this another passageway that Roman closed off?

And why does that question give me a sinking feeling?

I've seen movies where scientists lead a rat through a maze. The men in lab coats shift the cheese and walls just to see what'll happen. For the first time, I can understand how the rodent feels in these situations. Not good.

Voices echo through the shadows. Following the sound, I find that the trail does continue, only without the arrow markings from Roman. I keep on the trail until the passageway grows wider and brighter.

Then it ends.

Pausing, I give my eyes time to adjust to what feels like searing brightness. In reality, I stare out onto a grassy clearing that's bathed in moonlight. I exhale. Whatever that pathway was, it avoided Vision and the Darkness. I must have reached the mountain's exit, a place called the Fangs.

Looking up, I notice a pair of spikes jutting down from the cave's ceiling. Those shapes certainly do remind me of canines. A shiver of foreboding rolls across my shoulders.

I scan my surroundings more carefully. Beyond the Fangs, I spy a small clearing surrounded by a thick line of trees. Moonlight casts the scene in an eerie glow. No one appears to be nearby, but that can't be right. I just heard voices a few minutes ago. The hair on my neck prickles with awareness. I've been on enough missions to know what that means.

Hidden eyes watch me.

Best to stay on alert.

THE FANGS

23

MACK

Stepping forward, I march out from the cave and into the moonlight. Looking back, I see that there is indeed a shape carved into the mountain which resembles a fanged mouth. My pulse speeds. I passed by Vision and the Darkness.

What kind of reception am I walking into next?

Little by little, a dozen folks step out from the line of trees. I count adults of many ages and backgrounds. Some wear Roman togas; others sport jeans and T-shirts. All wear unreadable looks on their faces.

A jolt of worry moves through me. Do these people see me as a friend or foe? One way to find out.

I march up to the group and wait. Up close, these folks look pale and sickly. Many are far too thin. Some wear what can only be described as rags.

My heart cracks. These people have been trapped in a magical sphere for hundreds of years. With every passing day, their captors' poison—the dark water— makes them more ill.

"I'll do whatever I can to help you," I declare. "I promise."

24

KAPS

*N*ot my best plan.

In my defense, my family was being super supportive. I was heading off into a sketchy situation that involves vampire Nazis, so why not bring along all the help I can get? Plus, how badass would it be to march through a jungle with my family of magical warriors along for the journey?

In theory, it all sounded really cool.

In actual practice? Not so much.

Here's the situation. Pop Pops, AKA grandpa, AKA the General of the Angelic Army, brought along two thousand angelic warriors for my great entrance into El Dorado. Have you ever seen an angel try to fly under a canopy of tangly leaves and vines? It isn't pretty. Also, it turns out that monkeys are like magpies when they see white feathers. Half the angelic warriors now have simians on their backs.

The deal with the dragon shifters hasn't been much better. Our warriors began by marching in their human forms. Then massive snakes and a few growly jaguars got into the mix. From there, it's a reflex for my people to change into dragons. And you know what happens then? Hint: there's not a lot of room in the jungle for massive animals.

The dragons got stuck. Some also became too freaked out to shift back into their human shape.

It's a total clusterfuck.

I won't lie—it's also pretty funny. And I'd be giggling for sure, if it weren't for the fact that the portal to El Dorado is only open for an hour. All these snags are making us move far too slowly. A little part of me had hoped to see Mack at the gateway between Earth and this Wyvern realm, but now I'm thinking that's a long shot. Mack is a punctual guy.

Some small part of me points out that I could have tried harder to contact Mack and sync up. Now that my parents were on board, I didn't have to sneak around. And in fact, I did use a few enchantments to get a message across. I even texted Gage. When it didn't work, I dropped the whole thing like a hot brick. That same corner of my soul knows why I didn't try harder.

Mack would try to talk me out of this, and I really want to see El Dorado. I've obsessed with the place for years. Even if I see it for sixty seconds, that's worth the trouble.

So entering El Dorado is a requirement.

But bringing along an army wasn't.

Now I know.

At last, we reach the Divide. There's no missing this portal, considering how it's a loop of stone that sits above ground and glows blue.

I haul ass to the doorway and step through. Somehow, everyone I know is right behind me. Huntress tries to leap inside, but she gets blocked by the blue light.

My sister knocks on the barrier. "What's up with this thing?"

"It's Lady Aurelian's magic," I explain. "It doesn't let anyone through who can't help El Dorado."

Huntress' gaze turns deadly serious. "What kind of magic thinks I can't help?"

Much as I love Huntress' desire to help out and kick ass, I'm on a time schedule here. Still, everyone hauled their cookies through the freaking Amazon, so I need to give them a chance to join me.

And yes, I'd love the help. So I wait.

Next, Pop-Pops tries to step through. Nothing.

Mum. Nyet.

Da. No go.

And finally, Zin. That's a mega fail.

All in all, no one in my immediate family gets past the blue barrier. the next thing I know, Da starts lining up random angels and dragon warriors to try and enter. That's when I draw the line.

"Gotta run!" I call.

And I head off into the darkness.

More specifically, I make a beeline through the very large and obvious path through the cave. Turns out, it's hard to see in the dark without my heightened dragon senses. Which makes me go more slowly, but I still trudge forward.

In no time, I reach a far larger chamber that's lined with bones. A memory appears. Lady Aurelian said that sometimes folks found their way into the cave when the demon-titans were still awake.

Looks like those unfortunates ended up as lunch.

There's barely any light in here, but I'm getting pretty used to that by now. I step deeper into the cave.

A bright red dot appears. An old flashlight, maybe? With so many bones around, someone must have dropped gear before getting crunched. I take a second look.

Actually, that's not a point of crimson. My stomach tumbles. That thing is an eye.

One more opens.

And another.

Soon a dozen glowing eyes illuminate the chamber. The extra light makes another fact way clear.

Vision is awake.

Definitely.

Maybe.

Okay, I have no idea.

Sadly, the demon-titan just as badass as I remember from Nostra Quattro's simulation. Vision has a woman's body, insect-like head and great bat wings.

My stomach sinks. I wonder if she's hungry. Then I see the pile of bones under her feet. Thanks to the extra light, I can tell that there are way more dead things in here than I imagined.

Oh, this chick is hungry, all right. And I don't even see where her buddy is hiding. I'll just assume the Darkness is off chomping down a femur somewhere.

A voice screams inside my mind. Over and over, it howls the same two words.

Turn back!

It may be on to something.

VISION

2 5

KAPS

I stand at the entrance to the cavern of the demon-titans. Behind me, there waits my family and world. Up ahead, there's a freaky chick who stares forward with a kabillion eyes.

If this is how Vision sleeps, it's weird as Hell.

Although if she were awake, wouldn't she be gnawing on my skull right now? And she's not even the worst thing out here. Roman's probably trotting around El Dorado by now, making his Toxicant army and being an asshat in general.

Isn't there an old saying, *it's better to live another day than get eaten by a demon-titan?* There should be.

Yet for some reason, my feet feel rooted to this spot. I can't move forward, but I don't seem able to retreat either. Minutes tick by before a key question appears.

What would Great M do?

Once I picture the answer, I tiptoe into the main chamber. My pulse turns so fierce, I can feel my heart-beat in my throat. As I inch along, I try not to think about all the bones crunching under my feet. It isn't easy. For her part, Vision keeps staring with her googly bright eyes.

Did one of them blink?

Oh, no.

I think she's blinking.

Fuck it.

I run across the chamber at full speed, stopping only when I see a literal light at the end of the tunnel. The passageway turns into a skeletal cave mouth. I race into the moonlight, stop and brace my hands on my knees. For a while, it's all I can do to pull in more breaths.

Someone kneels before me. "Kaps, is that you?"

"Hey, Mack."

"I can't believe this. We had an understanding."

A group of Wyverns—all in their bipedal form—lurk on the other side of the clearing. Each one glares hot death in my direction. I gesture toward the group. "Are those friends of yours?"

"We're getting to know each other. They've never seen a dragon shifter before. That's why they're upset." Mack shakes his head. "Kaps, what are you doing here?"

"Whatever I can to help."

Snaps of stone sound behind me. Glancing over my shoulder, I see that the skull mouth is starting to close.

Mack points to the Fangs. "You need to leave."

I don't move. In this moment, it's all I can do.

Mack grips my upper arms. "Kaps, we talked about this. It's true that we have a rhana bond. But if you stay here, you'll grow to resent me. What we have is special. I won't see it destroyed. Plus, you can't shift. Roman could show up any second. Please don't risk your life over me."

I glance over to the cave's mouth. It's half-closed. I steel my spine and open my yap.

"Back in the cave, I saw Vision. That freak is scary as hell. I froze up and thought about running back home."

Mack shoots a nervous glance toward the closing jaws of the cave's mouth. "Why didn't you?"

"I wondered, *what would Great M do?* And that's when it hits me. Great M would say, *fuck Vision and the Darkness.* And she's right. You and I will take those two demons down. And we'll also crush Roman, too. End of story."

That's also the end of my speech. Not my greatest effort, but we'll see what Mack has to say.

MACK

*T*he mouth of the skull cave is three-quarters closed. Kaps simply must leave through it. I meet her gaze. When I next speak, I place all my soul into the words.

"Please, Kaps."

She slowly squares her shoulders. "I'll go if you want me to, but I believe in us. We can do this, Mack."

The moment freezes in time. Energy pulses between us. *The rhana bond.* To my eyes, Kaps seems encased in crimson fire. And my own skin glimmers with golden flame. Connection blazes between us. This bond has guided us throughout our lives, even when we didn't know it existed.

Suddenly, there's no question what I must do.

"Maybe we won't live through this," I state. "But I

know one thing for certain. I can't exist without knowing I gave our bond everything. Stay with me, Kaps. Let's do this."

"And?"

I can't help but smile. "I love you like crazy."

She winks. "I'm very lovable."

Behind us, the cave mouth grinds shut with a thud. It's over. We're together now, no matter what.

I wrap my arms around Kaps, ready to finally taste her lips and guide her body against mine. Little by little, I pull Kaps closer. Her warm breath cascades over my mouth.

Then a familiar voice breaks up the moment.

"You shouldn't have stayed away, little dragon."

That would be Mother.

Kaps and I step apart. Mother eyes my rhana with outright suspicion. "There are places we can hide you. That way, you won't distract my son."

I step between Mother and Kaps. "This woman is my rhana. She goes wherever she wants."

Mother lifts her shin. "Not while I am still queen."

"Look," I begin. "You said that your magic failed when it allowed Roman to enter El Dorado."

"I did."

"But what if the spell actually worked? Maybe Roman came through to El Dorado so a chain of events could result in me and Kaps doing more than just taking down Roman. We might destroy Vision and the Darkness as well. Maybe we're both here to set everyone free."

Mother narrows her eyes. "You're a clever boy when it comes to thinking on your feet. But that doesn't your words the truth."

"Doesn't make it false, either," I counter.

Mother pinches the bridge of her nose. "Fine. What do you suggest?"

I rub my palms together. "You know the territory and who the players are here. Kaps and I are experienced warriors. It'll take Roman a while to inject enough warriors to make a Toxicant army. While we wait, let's invest a little time and brainpower. Together, I know we all can come up with a solid plan."

And so, we start to scheme.

27

MACK

*H*ours tick by as we finalize our plan. Turns out, the folks in this clearing aren't actual fighters, apart from me and Kaps. The good news is that Lady Aurelian has two hundred people back in the city who are experienced warriors. She also has some ancient relics that we can use against Roman in his Toxicants.

Our first step is returning to the city of El Dorado. That way, we can pick up the relics as well as suit up the best warriors. But before we leave, I share my spare golden stake with Kaps. You'd think I gave my rhana a kitten, she's so excited.

As the last of us pack up, my heart soars. With every passing second, I feel more confident this is possible.

Kaps stands by my side. Our rhana bond has never been stronger. The plan with the Wyverns is rock solid.

We're about to march into the jungle when Mother pulls me and Kaps into a dual embrace.

"I am so happy to have you here. For the first time, I can see a future with my son." She turns to Kaps. "And his brilliant friend."

Kaps bobs her brows. "Let's end this."

I nod. "Time to take down some monsters."

Rustling noises erupt from the line of trees. A moment later, Roman steps into the clearing. He wears a black military uniform and a sly grin. All his wild white hair has been shaved away.

"Indeed, it is time to kill lesser creatures." Roman snaps his fingers. Hundreds of Toxicant warriors step out from the cover and into the moonlight.

Oh, no.

TOXICANT ARMY

28

KAPS

*a*t first, I can only focus one thing: a set of glowing eyes that stare at me from a skull-like face.

I've seen that particular look before. It was back at the Winter's Keep when I fought that Toxicant.

On reflex, I rub my shoulder where that vampire chomped into my skin… and took away my dragon. For the umpteenth time, I reach into my soul and search for the inner magic that brings my inner creature to life.

All I feel is hollowed out and cold. I blink hard, trying to keep the tears away. My dragon is gone.

I'm vaguely aware that the one Toxicant I've honed in on has more than a few buddies nearby. Soon, thousands of glowing eyes stare at me and Mack.

Not good.

Roman steps forward.

True confession. When I get stressed, I tend to hyper-focus on one little droplet of trouble instead of a full sea of awfulness. Just minutes ago, it was everything I could do soak in a single set of glowy-eyeballs in the jungle. Now, I'm getting overly interested in the growing amount of mud splatter on Roman's shiny knee-high boots.

Doesn't that bug him?

I glance down at my own shit-kickers. They are mud-splattered and completely appropriate for a mission in the jungle.

In all honestly, I could probably hyper-focus on Roman's boots for a few more minutes. Sadly, the guy has to go and open his big yap.

"Did you really think I'd give you a chance to organize against me?" Roman glares between me and Mack.

This is when I should shut up. But it's me.

I raise my hand. "In all honesty, I really thought that you'd give us plenty of planning time. I mean, you're wearing patent leather boots to a jungle fight. That's not the sign of a super-strategic thinker."

There. That told him.

Mack gives me a combination smile-n-side eye. He totally appreciates my humor. *Chalk one up for Kaps.*

Roman stalks closer to Mack, which isn't a safe

move. First of all, I'm very protective of my rhana. Second, I hate being ignored. I put a lot of effort into that *patent leather boot* crack. At the least, I deserve a classic bad guy response like, *Silence Wench!*

Now I'm really getting ticked.

"I've had decades to plan this attack," says Roman to Mack. "Ever hear of Blitzkrieg?"

"Um." I raise my hand higher. "Everyone's heard of Blitzkrieg."

Roman keeps on addressing someone who is *not me.* "Blitzkrieg means *lightning war.* The key is to strike quickly and with overwhelming strength. Blitzkrieg makes every enemy crumble."

I wave my hand in wide arcs. "Over here, Roman! Not sure if you caught the end of World War II, but Blitzkrieg didn't work out for you guys in the long run. It's hard to do anything quickly during winter in freaking Russia."

There. That told him, part two.

At last, Roman turns in my direction. Some small part of me points out that I'm hyper-focusing again. Only this time, instead of honing in on shiny boots, I'm getting overly excited about how often Roman talks to me.

And this small part of me has a point. But more of

me is really enjoying how Roman is back to acknowledging my existence.

"You criticize my plans?" asks Roman.

I lower my arm. Blood flow is starting to be an issue. "Yeah, I do."

"Yet you know nothing of them," declares Roman. "For instance, why did your parents agree to hand over *Mack's dead body* to me in exchange for your safety?"

In my book, this is great stuff. *Keep blabbing all your strategy, evil dude.*

"Let me think." I tap my chin in mock contemplation. "Because you tricked them into thinking Mack was horrible?"

"Yes, but that's not all."

I raise my pointer finger. "Before we move on to the rest of your amazing plan." And here, I use said pointer finger along with other digits to make air quotes as I speak the words *amazing plan.* "Your whole scheme was to make my parents hate and murder Mack. That did not work. And why were you a total failure?" Here I throw in some more chin tapping because I'm on a roll. "Because I asked my parents to spare his life. They didn't listen to your lies because they trusted me more."

Mack punches the air. "Harrumph."

I give him an air kiss. "Thanks, babe."

At this point, I realize how all the Wyverns and humans in the clearing are now staring at our little conversation with opened mouths and bugged-out eyes. As for Lady Aurelian, the woman is the definition of unwell.

"Indeed, your parents spared Mack's life," continues Roman. "Yet that was all part of my plan."

"Really." I drag out the word.

"Please," states Roman. "I didn't expect anyone to kill Mack that day. My goal was to make your parents aware of your secret life murdering vampires. Once that was out in the open, it started a chain reaction that brought everyone to this very spot. You see, if I'd just sent Mack an invitation, he'd have been far more prepared."

I scrunch up my mouth and think this through. *Damn.* Roman might be onto something. Ever since I found that Wyvern scepter in the Hexenwing Museum, things have been happening too quickly to analyze.

My stomach tumbles. The scepter.

"You." I point at Roman.

He grins, and the expression is more smug than ever. "Me?"

"You had one of your vampires take on the appearance of Mistress Cerys' guards. That was why the Hexenwings sent Huntress a dozen invitations for the museum tour. You wanted me to go. And that scepter was the only non-dusty thing in the case. Your agent planted it for me to find."

"Indeed, you did everything to my schedule," agrees Roman. "I needed your help so Mack would talk to this creature—" Here Roman gestures toward Lady Aurelian "—And get her to convince you both to enter El Dorado. And so you did."

Angry energy streams through me. I lock gazes with Mack while nodding toward Roman. The thought is there if unspoken. *Should we attack?*

Mack shakes his head slightly while tapping his ear. I get the message. *No, we should listen.*

Which makes sense. *Too bad I can't punch the old vampire just once in the throat.*

Mack gestures between us. "Why must both of us be here? It's not like you need help gathering dark water."

"Why?" A wild look takes over Roman's face. "WHY?" The old vampire rounds on Lady Aurelian. "You didn't tell them?"

The queen lifts her chin. "No."

Roman leans back and laughs his ass off. I'm talking a classic, over-the top display of maniacal hilarity.

I roll my eyes. "Any time now, drama boy."

At last, Roman stops his mwah-hah-hah fiesta. "I'll tell you why I want you both here. Revenge."

"Quiet, you bastard," yells Lady Aurelian.

I do a double-take. Lady Aurelian is the type of queen that you'd expect to use words like *waste product* instead of *poop*. I can't believe she just said *bastard.*

"Rot in hell," adds Lady Aurelian. "I'm the one who deserves revenge."

Roman points between me and Mack. "You're both here to listen to the truth."

"I will fight you before you say a word," announces Lady Aurelian. "I've done it before."

"I doubt that," says Roman. "You expended way too much energy yesterday in contacting Mack. Now you're weak as a newborn. And that was all part of my plan, too."

Lady Aurelian pales. The truth is obvious. She really is unable to fight.

Mack steps forward. "If you have something to say, then speak."

"As you command," announces Roman.

My heart sinks. I hate to admit this, but I underestimated Roman. His super-sneaky plans are actually pretty good, even if he doesn't appreciate how to care for fine footwear. Whatever's coming up next, I'm pretty sure of one thing.

It's going to suck.

29

MACK

*a*ll my life, Roman was the closest thing I had to a father. That was all a lie. Now he wants to share his big revenge.

Bring it on. What could be worse than a lifetime of hate?

Roman meets my gaze. "Don't you wonder who your father is?"

I shrug. "You always told me I was left on the doorstep of the Zoetic Fortress. Lady Aurelian shared that she's my mother. So go for it. Shatter me. Who is my father?"

"His name is Lucas," adds Roman. "Ring any bells?"

"A few," I reply. "It's a common enough name."

Memories appear. When Kaps and I were in the simulation from Nostra Quattro, the young version of

Roman mentioned someone named Lucas. At the time, I figured it was a random Nazi warrior.

Roman rounds on Lady Aurelian. "What about you? Do you wish to explain?"

Mother keeps staring at the ground. Her chest twitches with held-in sobs, yet she doesn't say a word. I get the feeling it's a lot for her to just stay vertical.

"Lucas was my brother." Roman points to Lady Aurelian. "And this one killed him by luring him away from our unit." Roman paces a line across the darkened grounds. "It all started with a command from Hitler himself. Our Fuhrer collected magical items. He'd heard about El Dorado and its dark water. I was sent off to find this magical liquid. And so I did."

"You don't understand what we lost," continues Roman. "The war was almost over. American tanks were driving across my homeland. If I could have gotten enough dark water, I could have created an army of super-soldiers to help us win. But instead, I wasted precious time arguing with Lucas."

Roman's mouth thins to an angry line. "By the time we left El Dorado with the dark water, Hitler had already taken his own life. It was over. And all because my brother believed this nonsense that he's found his rhana. His life mate. Lucas said he knew it from the first moment he laid eyes on Lady Aurelian."

"Thus began my long planning," declares Roman. "Every fifteen years, I came back for more dark water… but also to save Lucas. And when I finally found my brother? He was holding you. A little abomination. And my own flesh and blood fought me to the death over you. I had to kill Lucas, you see. He wouldn't give you up."

"Murderer," whispers Lady Aurelian.

"I'm only what you made me into," counters Roman. "You used witchcraft to entrap my brother. You ruined my chance to win World War II. Ever since then, I've plotted to build a better army of Toxicants that will regain everything I lost in the war. And to destroy my first creations—those faulty Audax—I raised Mack to be a Zoetic warrior."

This is too much. "So while I was off fighting Audax, you were in the lab building a better version of those same vampires?"

"Exactly. And now we're here. I have my new Toxicant army. And I did more than create my new warriors. I also schemed how to bring them into El Dorado quickly and transform them into vampires more so far, you could ever imagine it was happening. Blitzkrieg."

A heavy sense of loathing settles into my bones. "All those missions you sent me on over the years. You had me test transporter technology and rapid injections… that was all in preparation for this day."

Roman nods slowly. "And the best part was this: I made you love me for it."

With those words, something inside me snaps. The Roman I knew was an illusion. The monster before me just wants to feed off and pain. Knowing that, a deep sense of calm washes through me.

We'll see who gets revenge.

"Let's recap," says Kaps. I'm beyond happy to report that my woman speaks those two words with no small amount of sass. "Roman, you think Lucas betrayed you… so you make his son, Mack, assist your revenge plans … when in reality, all your brother really did was fall in love. Please, take this the *wrong* way. You put a lot of effort in here, and yet you still look pretty miserable."

I really do adore this woman.

"I'm not done yet," counters Roman. "Once Lady Aurelian is dead, I shall become the rightful ruler of El Dorado. After all, I *am* the king's only heir."

Little by little, Roman swings his gaze toward my mother. I've been in enough battles to know what Roman's thinking.

Pure murder gleams in eyes.

30

KAPS

hile Roman was blabbing all his strategy, I felt like I had my head on again. Sure, I got a little distracted by his boots, but that ended up working itself into a nice little insult, so I still consider that a win.

Then things start moving so fast, I can't track what's happening.

Suddenly, the full Toxicant army rushes out of the jungle. Twenty monsters tackle Mack. At the same time, Roman raises his right arm. White light glows in his palm for a moment, then a scepter appears in his fist.

Roman stalks toward Lady Aurelian. The poor woman is still working hard to stay upright.

"Can't cast a single spell, can you?" Roman chuckles. "You aren't even strong enough to breathe golden fire.

What good is a Wyvern royal who can't access your special powers just when you need them most?"

My heart cracks. I keep forgetting how different things are for Wyverns. For dragons, anyone in the Firelord tribe can breathe flame. It's trickier for Wyverns. Only the top royals can breathe golden fire. So Roman's rubbing it in that Lady Aurelian can't do much of anything right now.

What a dick.

There is good news, though. Unlike Mack, I've got two Toxicants racing in my direction. It's insulting, really. Still, I'll take my good luck where I can find it. If Roman doesn't consider me a big threat, he's about to get an education.

At first, I reach out to my inner dragon. That's an automatic response whenever I face an attack. Even if I don't transform, it's good to know my dragon side is there and ready.

Only she's not.

So I move onto Plan B. I pull out my golden stake and spike the first Toxicant through the chest. The second vampire tries to grab me from behind, but the guy clearly hasn't had an experience with tails. Once I'm done with attacker number one, I toss my stake over my shoulder. My tail grabs the golden spike in its arrowhead-shaped end and stabs vampire number two through the heart.

With those two vamps down, I race toward Lady Aurelian. For his part, Roman points his scepter right at Mack's mother. Clearly, Roman wants to kill the queen and take over El Dorado.

I must stop him.

MACK

One thing I'll say for Toxicants, they move incredibly fast.

Before I know what's happening, twenty of them surround me. Some pin my legs; others go for my arms. Even more sink their teeth into my flesh. Each bite is laced with poison. My vision blurs. Energy wanes. Consciousness starts to fade.

Somewhere in this nightmare, I hear my mother's voice. "Save my son!"

Toxicants get yanked off me. Others crumple over as golden stakes are jammed through their chests. It takes me a minute to realize what's happening.

The Wyverns and humans have joined the battle. These folks aren't trained warriors, but what they lack in experience, they make up for in determination.

Someone hands me a healing potion. Normally, I'd ask a few questions before downing a strange elixir. This time, I finish it in a single gulp.

My head clears as I take in the scene. The Wyverns now stand in their winged forms. By lining up side by side, the massive creatures create a shield between me and the Toxicant army. My eyes widen as I soak in their true shape. Each Wyvern stands about ten feet tall. They may not breathe fire, but they can all attack with jagged claws and sharp teeth. Totally badass.

More of Roman's Toxicants pour out of the jungle. The Wyverns are fighting well, but it's obvious there are way too many Toxicants.

At this point, it's tempting to act first and think later, but I've been on many missions where that ends in disaster. Instead, I take a moment to soak in my surroundings. What I see heats my blood with rage.

Lady Aurelian lays on her side, immobile. Kaps stands between my unconscious mother and a very angry Roman. Meanwhile, Roman holds his magical scepter like a baseball bat. Bringing the staff down, Roman smashes the weapon against the side of Kaps' head. My rhana crumples to the ground.

And I lose my mind.

Before, I'd seen a light haze of golden light envelops my skin. Now my entire body blazes golden fire.

Connections form inside me. Powers align. Energies become unleashed.

I begin to change.

Moments ago, my body had been riddled with bite marks. Now those wounds heal up before my eyes. Sinews snap. Wings take shape. Scales appear. Muscles grow. The fiery magic that surrounds my body now shoots up to the skies. A slice of sunlight breaks through the eternal darkness

I become the Wyvern Macaidan.

MACAIDAN

MACK

I take to the skies, swooping over the clearing. Without being ordered, my people wing up and follow my lead. As I grasp Toxicants in my talons, the gold of my royal magic acts like the metal itself. The Toxicants scream in pain before dissolving into dust.

After clearing off the battlefield, I take to the jungle beyond, tearing up trees and uncovering Toxicants. Each meets the same fate.

With the army out of commission, I swoop back to the clearing and land before Kaps and Lady Aurelian. My Wyvern senses are keen. Instantly, I know that these two are both unconscious, but alive.

I turn to Roman.

"Any last words?" My Wyvern's voice bellows across

the jungle. Which makes sense, considering I'm twice the size of any other Wyvern. "You didn't plan for this, did you? After so much hatred of rhana bonds, you never thought the magic of fated mates would release my inner monster."

"No, I didn't see this," says Roman. "But I did fear that Lady Aurelian would give me trouble. So I do have one final failsafe. It's certain to stop you."

Roman slams his scepter down onto the ground. White lightning shoots out from his staff, filling the clearing with brightness. The pale energy slams right into the side of the mountain. The skull-like cave entrance collapses. Ear-splitting booms shake the air. The ground rumbles. Animals screech to the skies. The entire mountain face splits open.

Vision and the Darkness rise from the shattered rock. She still appears as a humanoid with insect head and bat wings. He's a massive creature with a stout body and a face made of tentacles.

Roman points to me. "There he is. The new Wyvern royal! You must destroy him."

"Destroy," repeats Vision. All her eyes stare in one direction: me.

A single thought appears in my mind. *I have no idea how to fight these two.*

33

KAPS

The first thing I'm aware of is pain. It's not mine. Hurt careens down my limbs. Every inch of my skin burns with agony. The deepest part of my soul cries out.

Wake up! Mack needs you!

Blinking hard, I force my eyes to open. The sight that greets me is one that'll haunt me for a lifetime. Which, based on how this battle is going, won't be very long.

Vision and Darkness take turns attacking Mack. His Wyvern self lies curled up on the clearing. Scales are torn off. One eye is swollen shut. A great gash extends along his rib cage.

Mack doesn't have much longer.

There's some good news in all this badness. Lady

Aurelian still lies nearby, unconscious but alive. Even better, there are small piles of blue ash all over the green. While I was out of it, the Toxicant army was destroyed. Chances are, Mack took care of those vampires. Sadly, the battlefield is also littered with the corpses of Wyverns. Based on the large claw marks through the dead, I'm guessing it was Vision and the Darkness who took down Mack's people.

My attention snaps again to my rhana. Golden fire surrounds Mack's body. I remember that effect. It's something I saw in my mind when Mack and I would connect through our rhana bond. Now it's in reality and surrounding Mack. Protecting him.

Trouble is, the fire is also dying out. Unless I do something fast, Vision and the Darkness will destroy my rhana.

An idea appears.

I don't have my dragon, but I still do have a magical connection to the man I love. It's power that can do just about anything. Closing my eyes, I tap into my feelings for Mack. I picture his lopsided smile and hear his deep laughter. I recall the heat of his kisses and the gentle sunshine of his embraces. The magic of our rhana bond us flares to life in my soul.

I open my eyes. Across the clearing, the Darkness

rakes its slimy claws down Mack's spine. The intensity of my love now burns into something else. Red-hot fury churns through me.

My dragon awakens.

KAPS

34

MACK

*M*y soul hovers in a place between agony and death. Vision and the Darkness claw and bite my Wyvern body. Pain radiates through every nerve ending. Yet along with that hurt, there comes the peace of knowing it will all end soon.

Waves of heat move over me. Vision and the Darkness cease their attacks. I force myself to turn over and face the clearing.

That when I see her.

Kaps.

She's in her dragon form and breathing crimson fire. It's her heat that I felt over me before; her blasts of flame sent off the demon-titans.

Vision and the Darkness haven't gone far, though. The pair still lurk on the edges of the burned-out jungle, waiting for their chance to destroy us both for good.

Kaps spreads her great wings and speeds over to my side.

"Mack," she cries. "Can you hear me?"

"Yes." It takes another effort, but I get myself onto all fours. "I'm ready to fight."

"My flames drive the demon-titans away, but don't finish them off. I have an idea. Maybe if we tap into our rhana magic—and combine our fire—then we might take them down."

As Kaps speaks, I see that familiar illusion of red flame dancing across her skin. The fire illuminates her, yet doesn't burn. In that moment, I know Kaps is right. We can do this.

With that realization, more golden fire moves across my skin as well. Our rhana magic. My injuries heal. Scales regrow. Muscles knit back together. My wings become whole again. Power and energy move through me, fast as lightning.

I force my battered arms to extend. Breathing deeply, I tap into the fire that hides within me.

Vision takes to the skies. The Darkness turns semi-transparent. While still in its misty shape, the second demon-titan moves toward the clouds as well.

Kaps and I pump our wings and chase after them.

The demon-titans swirl and dive around us, trying to sink in their claws or teeth.

Moving in unison, my rhana and I let loose our inner fire. My flames shine like liquid gold. Hers dance in shades of deep red. We angle our blasts so our efforts combine. A new blaze forms that mixes red and gold, metal and flame. The combined fire tears through Vision first. The demon titan lets out a howl of pain before burning down to nothing but bones.

Next we turn to the Darkness. This demon-titan moves faster, since he's now more of a shadow than anything. Still, our combined blast singes his cloudy body into vapor. Within minutes, all that remains of the Darkness is a worm-like husk that tumbles to the ground.

Kaps and I soar back to the clearing. Hope and pride sparks in my chest. I search the expanse grass for my mother.

I find her laying on the ground, unconscious. Roman leans over her while holding a dagger to her throat. A single line of blood trickles down her skin.

"You won't hurt me," declares Roman. "Unless you want her dead."

Of all Roman's plans, this one is the worst. Taking in a deep breath, I exhale a line of golden flame at Mother. Roman leaps back, afraid of being burned. But Wyvern fire could never hurt another royal. My blaze presses Mother well out of Roman's reach.

Dropping his dagger, Roman raises his hands in surrender. "This is all a misunderstanding." He focuses on Kaps. "You're part thrax, aren't you? That means you have rules of battle. You can't strike unless I'm attacking you."

"Thrax are part angel," says Dragon Kaps. "I am not."

"Fine, we'll do this another way." Roman extends his arm. A scepter appears in his fist once more. Roman slams the staff against the ground. Waves of violet energy curl up his body.

Now it's Roman's turn to transform. He expands into a hulking beast that resembles a Toxicant, except Roman's version has four arms, two heads and stands as tall as the mountain.

I turn to Dragon Kaps. "I'll get a stake, you distract him."

"With pleasure." Kaps takes to the skies. Once she's close enough to Roman, she flies by while breathing fire. As Monster Roman roars in pain, charred lines appear on his blue skin.

At the same time, I wing off toward the undamaged part of the jungle. Once there, I find a tall tree which I encase in golden flame. Unlike my battle fire, this blast is *the Breath of Midas.* As my flames touch the tree, it changes into solid gold.

Grasping the metal trunk in my jaws, I pull it from the ground. With my new weapon in hand, I speed back to the battlefield. Dragon Kaps still flies circles around Monster Roman. I snap my head and send my weapon flying. The golden stake pierces Roman through the heart. He crumples in on himself, moaning. Within seconds, all that's left of the man is just another pile of ashes.

At last.

35

MACK

Roman, the Toxicants, and even the demon-titans... they're all gone. Cool relief washes over me as I return to my human form. My body armor is shredded, but that's a small price to pay. Kaps transforms as well. Her clothes made it through pretty much unscathed. I'll have to ask her how she managed that trick later.

For now, I pull my rhana into my arms. "Are you hurt?"

"No, I'm fine."

Around us, the landscape changes. Before, I was able to send some power into the skies. A single patch turned blue. Now a full and yellow sun burns away all the clouds. The jungle regrows. Where water used to sit in dark puddles, now it runs gold.

Mother rises. I'm beyond happy to see how color has returned to her skin. She kneels by a thin rivulet of golden water and scoops some of the precious liquid into her mouth.

"Ah," says Mother. "You've no idea how much better this feels."

The other Wyverns and humans follow Mother's lead. If dark water poisoned them, then this golden version heals.

Mother steps over to me and Kaps. My rhana bows her head. "I'm sorry for all those you lost."

Sure enough, many Wyvern bodies cover the clearing. Mother scans them all, then lifts her arm. Once again, a scepter appears in her fist. Mother slams the staff onto the ground. All the Wyvern bodies vanish.

"Where did they go?" I ask.

"Into magical stasis," replies Mother. "Once I'm stronger, I'll fully heal them. They weren't dead for long enough for it to become permanent."

I lift my brows. "Healing the recently dead? That's really something."

"Think that's impressive?" asks Mother. "Wait until you see what my magic does now. I'd always hoped to see this part of my spell come to life. Now I shall."

Back in Nostra Quattro's simulation, Kaps and I saw El Dorado get transported inside a glittering sphere of gold. Now that bubble appears once more. It blots out the sun and surrounds everything in a golden hue.

Once again everything rises. This time, Kaps and I know what to expect. We hold on to each other as the ground rumbles and the world moves. Our bubble of El Dorado shoots high into the air before careening back to the ground. We slam down onto a familiar spot.

The Auric Badlands.

The golden city reforms around Kaps' gray tower. Across the badlands, dry rock crumbles as trees burst up from the earth. All around the tower, empty ground becomes a teeming jungle. The air turns warm and wet. A golden river flows out from El Dorado and into the jungle beyond.

Mother beams. "I am home again."

Kaps' people file out from the tower and walk about in wonder. Wyverns and humans descend from their golden buildings to stare at the clear blue sky. Cheers rise up.

That is, until the skies turn dark once more.

Mother steps over to Kaps. "What's that?" She gestures toward what looks like a solid black cloud that hurtles toward us.

"Those are angels and dragons," Kaps replies with a smile. "A lot of them."

"Don't worry," I add. "They're family."

36

KAPS

*W*hat happens next is pure chaos and I love it. My parents arrive to greet me and Mack. Representatives from all the great tribes land and give their congratulations. Some fast thinkers even bring welcome gifts for the returned Wyverns.

Somehow, Ndidi joins us as well. The whole thing turns into a huge party that lasts for hours. My parents conjure a massive meal while Pop-Pops entertains everyone with precision flying stunts from his angelic troops.

Eventually, I find Zin and Huntress in the crowd. We share the mother of all bear hugs.

Zin steps back. "I knew you could do it, Kaps."

Huntress punches me on the shoulder. "And your dragon is back."

"How can you tell?" I ask.

"You're smiling," she replies.

And that is true.

Huntress forces a grin of her own before slipping away into the crowd. My heart goes out to her. She misses Gage something terrible. Still, I don't know how much longer she can hold out. It isn't wise to fight a rhana bond. And Mistress Cerys did have that prophecy about ogres. Who knows what can happen?

All in all, it seems like Great M is right. Our family always works things out in the end.

MACK

The cheering and dancing goes on well into the next day. Kaps and I hold hands through it all. Someone constructs a stage in the center of El Dorado. It's clear that the platform is new, considering how it's the only thing around which isn't made of gold. Mother guides me and Kaps onto the stage.

Once the three of us stand atop the platform, the celebrating crowd becomes quiet. Mother raises her hand; a golden crown materializes on her palm. She turns to me.

"Do you accept the rule of all Wyverns?"

This isn't very formal. In fact, I still wear the equivalent of battle rags. Yet as I'm quickly learning, this is the classic Wyvern way of things. My people value celebration over ceremony.

"Yes," I reply.

Mother sets the crown atop my head and then turns to the masses. Every inch of El Dorado seems to be packed with happy partygoers.

"All hail Macaidan Vasiliás the Tenth, King of the Wyverns!"

The crowd takes up the chant. "All hail! All hail!"

Mother raises her arm; the mob falls silent once more. She turns to Kaps. "And what about you? Ready for a crown?"

I get what Mother means here. Kaps and I are not that old. It's a lot to become a ruler. I lean in closer to my woman. "Do whatever you want," I whisper. "I'll still be here."

Kaps rolls her eyes. "Hey, we're already rhanas. I'd say becoming a queen is pretty minor in the grand scheme of things." She turns to Mother. "I'm ready."

Mother lifts her hand. Another gold crown materializes on her palm. Mother sets it atop Kaps' head.

"All hail, Kaps, Queen of the Wyverns!"

Again the crowd takes up the call. "All hail! All hail!" From here, the cheers dissolve into much dancing and drinking. My people could teach frat boys how to have a good time.

While the crowd moves on, I pull Kaps flush against me and press my lips to hers. At last, we share a full kiss.

And as of this moment, I now have a family, a future and a name. This is more joy than I could ever have dreamed possible.

And the best part? I'll share it all with my rhana.

—The End—

The adventure continues with HUNTRESS, Angelbound Offspring #7!

*T*he adventure continues with HUNTRESS, Angelbound Offspring #7!

About HUNTRESS

Princess. Warrior. Dragon Shifter. Huntress.

When it comes to protecting her family, eighteen-year-old Princess Huntress is known for kicking ass, taking names and then kicking a little more ass, just to be sure. She's the last of her kind—a glass dragon shifter —and no matter what the threat, Huntress always tracks it down solo.

Then Huntress meets the leader of the L'Griffe crime

family, Gage Beaufort, who is a dashing dragon shifter with a knee-melting stare. The attraction is instant, yet Huntress hates it. Why? Crime syndicates hurt royal authority, which means they threaten her family. Long story short, being with Gage is just wrong. Besides Huntress already has a rock-solid life plan, and that's to fight alone, forever. No relationships, thank you very much.

But when a new danger threatens the royals, everything changes.

Now Huntress needs a mercenary army and fast, so she forges an alliance with L'Griffe. To protect those she loves, Huntress agrees to marry someone she loathes: Gage Beaufort. But will the extra help be enough?

Even worse, Huntress' family isn't the only thing at risk--the same is true for the princess' heart. Because Gage is a man who always gets what he wants. In this case, the crime lord desires Princess Huntress, body and soul.

"With Angelbound Offspring, every page is entertaining... an exciting story that unfolds with magic, dragons, a little romance and a villain to despise." – *Tonja, Goodreads*

Angelbound Offspring

1. Maxon
2. Portia
3. Zinnia
4. Rhodes
5. Kaps
6. Mack
7. Huntress

ALSO BY CHRISTINA BAUER

HUNTRESS

The adventure continues with HUNTRESS, Angel-bound Offspring #7!

FAIRY TALES OF THE MAGICORUM

A modern fairy tale that *USA Today* calls a 'must-read!' Check out WOLVES AND ROSES!

ANGELBOUND

Check out ANGELBOUND, the kick-ass paranormal romance! Read on for a sample...

PIXIELAND DIARIES

PIXIELAND DIARIES tells the story of sassy pixie Calla and 'her' elf prince, Dare.

DIMENSION DRIFT

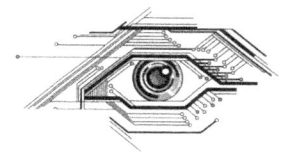

A kick-ass heroine + a swoon-worthy prince + an all-girl heist = SCYTHE!!!

BEHOLDER

Medieval mages ... Slow-burn love ... And heart-pounding action! Check out the BEHOLDER series!

APPENDIX

ABOUT CHRISTINA BAUER

Christina Bauer thinks that fantasy books are like bacon: they just make life better. All of which is why she writes romance novels that feature demons, dragons, wizards, witches, elves, elementals, and a bunch of random stuff that she brainstorms while riding the Boston T. Oh, and she includes lots of humor and kick-ass chicks, too. Christina lives in Newton, MA with her husband, son, and semi-insane golden retriever, Ruby.

Stalk Christina on Social Media

Blog:
http://monsterhousebooks.com/blog/
category/christina

Facebook:
https://www.facebook.com/authorBauer/

Instagram:
https://www.instagram.com/christina_cb_bauer/

Twitter:
@CB_Bauer

VLOG:
https://tinyurl.com/Vlogbauer

Web site:
www.bauersbooks.com

IF YOU ENJOYED THIS BOOK...

...Please consider leaving a review, even if it's just a line or two. Every bit truly helps, especially for those of us who don't *write by the numbers,* if you know what I mean. Plus I have it on good authority that every time you review an indie author, somewhere an angel gets a mocha latte. For reals.

And angels need their caffeine, too.

ACKNOWLEDGMENTS

If you're reading my freaking acknowledgements, chances are, I should thank you for something. So, for the record: you are awesome, dear reader.

That said, huge and heartfelt thanks must go out to my husband and son for their rock-solid support. Writing books means a lot of early mornings, late nights, long weekends, and never-ending patience. You two are the best guys in the universe, period.

After that, I must thank the extensive network of reviewers, friends and colleagues who helped me build my writing chops in general. Gracias.

Finally, deep affection goes out to my late, much loved, and dearly missed Aunt Sandy and Uncle Henry. You saw the writer in me, always. Thank you, first and last.

BEVERLY HILLS VAMPIRE

**A NOVELLA BY
CHRISTINA BAUER**

www.ingramcontent.com/pod-product-compliance
Lightning Source LLC
Chambersburg PA
CBHW051430170626
46809CB00006B/2397